The Potato Fields

Cornelius Doherty

The Potato Fields
Cornelius Doherty

ISBN: 978-0-6484152-3-7

First published 2026.
Published by: Self-published.

For Martin
'Who goes there, friend or foe?'
Bridie, Johnny and a man called Joe
Irish storytellers
Alex King
Thank You

Glossary

Weans
Children

Dolmen
Celtic burial structure

Perdies
Potatoes

A wheen
A few

Killybegs
Donegal fishing village

Wallsteads
stone remains of old house or structure

Gurnin'
Whinging

Black clocks
Black beetles

Crabbit
Cranky

Schoch
Drain or open trench

Knock
Irish pilgrimage town in Mayo

Scunnered
Annoyed — bored

Craic
fun

Thran
Stubborn — awkward person

Not a titter of wit
No common sense

The potatoes were set. Carefully hand laid, one foot apart in straight drills. They rested briefly in fertile Irish soil before beginning their journey to the light and life itself until harvest time. The farmer stood back, feeling proud. A vision appeared. A young man with his back to her walked over the drills for a short time and she knew the sign. He looked over his left shoulder and saw her watching. He waved his hand in farewell and carried on for a time towards a white mist that had appeared by the stand of hazelnut and birch trees in the corner of the field. He stopped suddenly and looked back again, this time she could see the expression on his face, and he smiled. Turning around, he walked back towards her, his face beaming with love and his bright green eyes shone under dark, heavy brows. The drills were undamaged, straight, sharp and pointy. His steps light, taken in the other world, seen here. His time would come, but not today.

Introduction

My name is Big George. When I left the land of the living as you know it, I had seven children, with one gone before me, and twenty-eight grandchildren. Mostly, they were hard work: they annoyed my happiness with their loud and noisy behaviour. Unruly weans left doors open to allow in dogs and draughts, their high-pitched screams echoed off the whitewashed walls of my farmhouse like bells clanging for the evening Angelus. I will admit to being none too patient with any of them, taking little joy in their presence and turning my hearing aid down for the most part as I got older. I was always glad to see them gone home, be that somewhere in Donegal or Derry or England, made no odds to me so long as I was left in peace and my wife in a reasonable mood. I wasn't known for my outward showing of affection. Some say I died of a hardened heart brought on by years of being hard and stubborn, or thran, as the locals called it, like a shit carter's horse. It wasn't until I passed into the light and calm of the afterlife that I realised what I was missing out on.

Hard hearts were created by hard times. Ploughing fields with thran, stubborn horses, hitting sharp stones in small fields to crack the plough and break a man's back. Cutting turf, corn, hay, working cattle, turnips and potatoes, more bastard potatoes than you could poke a stick at, not only broke my back but, at the rear, broke my heart as well. I take some responsibility for my insolence, but not all. God had a lot to do with it. He gave me the theatre in the valley of tears, as well as the cast and the backdrop, but it was my performance and mine alone from start to finish, something I have only just come to realise, laid out here with two empty pockets and nothing to take with me but Atlantic air. I was both the director and the star of the show, and as the curtain fell and the crowd applauded, there were others, many others, that sat silently and asked for a refund, wishing they had neither seen the show nor been cast a part within it.

I wanted a second chance, just another couple of weeks and I'd tell them all that I loved them. As I passed over, I was granted the wish to follow one of my grandchildren, to direct all this newfound love from beyond the veil. I was granted this wish for one and one only, but at no time could I interfere, open doors, advise or help. I could observe and send love, and I chose John Devenney, my grandson. John was fourteen at the time and was not yet affected by the world around him.

I had strict instructions to be ready for the light in three days' time and not an hour more. The show was over and there was to be no encore. As luck would have it, earthly time meant nothing to me now. Years could drift by like seconds on a timekeeper's watch and I had all the time in the world, the duration of John's life.

And so, with all the love in the world and so much more from the universe, I recount this tale now.

Chapter 1

Sunday, 15th March 1981 3:00pm.

The Parish, Buncrana, County Donegal, Ireland

The fire in the kitchen was red hot — full of hard black turf from Augaweel hill. Had I been there, I'd have roared that there was no need for the half of it. Pure waste of good turf and them being so hard to dry in a wet year, not to mention blowing up the cooker into the bargain. They never listened anyway, and I was well past caring. There was a big crowd for my wake, and they filed past me in all their sorrow, marvelling at me laid out in my Sunday, wedding and funeral best for all to see. They touched my lifeless hands and dropped the odd Mass card at my feet, bringing the cold and damp of the Sunday evening with them. For the first time in my life/afterlife, the draught didn't bother me, and lucky it didn't because I couldn't shout for someone to close the door anyway. The heat from the fire drove out the March wind with gusto like a blacksmith's bellows, fanning a warm breath onto the cold, grey street.

"Sorry for yer troubles, aye, aye, aye, surely to God", they went through the repertoire of usual wake clichés, enough to pass themselves, saying something and nothing at the same time.

"He went quick at the rear, God knows right enough, wasn't he a wild big man too, and very like himself there, looks well though aye aye aye", they swished, almost whispering in quiet reverence to my mournful family and mimed a quick prayer before mingling. The open fire in the lower room could melt a chimney pot and very nearly warmed me back to life. Weans walked around the plush 'good room' carpet with the kettle of tea and plates of fresh cut sandwiches, while on a fancy China plate was a spread of Carrolls, Major and Woodbine cigarettes.

Cissy McGoldrick lived between my house and Stragill shore and was a far-out cousin of mine. Her thatched house was nestled amongst hazelnut, birch trees and blackberry bushes below the Planting. Few people walked there after dark and, if they did, they had hackles on their backs like a horse's mane. Cissy lived alone there in a small clearing, sheltered from the northern storms by the forest and the undergrowth. She relished the lively wake and the chance to get chatting to the neighbours and speak in a posh accent to strangers. She grabbed the tray with the milk and sugar and walked behind the young girl pouring the tea from the big grey kettle. With her black hands, red ruddy face and tight black curly hair, seeing her like this made me laugh so hard that I almost woke up. The girl had just poured a black cup for Jim Gill.

"Plenty a milk for ye Jim", she poured half the jug into the cup, turning his black tea into a cup of snow.

"Plenty a sugar for ye, Jim", she started digging into the bowl with a heaped spoon ready.

"I'm grand, no, I don't take sugar this long time", Jim replied.

"What? No sugar, take sugar, plenty a sugar here and more in the press."

Jim remonstrated and put his hand over the top of the cup in refusal. He was annoyed about the milk, but he'd drink the tea and get a better cup in a while. As he looked away to take a sandwich off the plate, she dumped two quick spoonfuls into his cup and stirred the white tea like she was churning milk with a paddle.

"Sweet mother of Holy Jesus", Jim gasped, and the sweat rolled from his forehead. Cissy continued and gave milk and sugar to everyone, whether they wanted it or not. It was the best day of her life, and my soul laughed hard, so hard in fact, that the hardness around my heart began to melt and fade away. I was enjoying the craic at my own wake. My grandson John worked for Cissy in the evenings for a pound a week and a dozen soft-shelled eggs, cleaning out byres, feeding cows or carrying water from the white stone well. I hoped that the time I was to spend with him would, in some way, counterbalance what he could become if he spent any more time with her.

Pat Gavin, a tall spindly neighbour with a craggy sharp chin and black greasy hair stood with his back to the fire, scraping chocolate biscuits and egg and onion sandwich from his rotten teeth before he lit up next to me. He stopped John in the middle of the best carpeted floor and put a further two Woodbine smokes behind each ear for later.

For some strange reason, I could read his thoughts and he smiled at me, knowing that I would have wasted neither an egg and onion sandwich or a cigarette on this man. I had a saying in life 'you'll shite when your belly's full' and I threw it at him. He stared at me knowingly and his shoulders hunched over with a shiver — hailstones fell down his back, knowing that I was watching him, even in death. He edged closer to the fire to get warm again and his greasy hair melted. The smell of cow dung, sheep dip and byre wafted around him, and the crowd parted like a biblical parable. On cue, Father Doherty ducked his head inside the front door, and they started praying the Rosary for my soul's intention and safe passage, Pat Gavin and all. My soul was already exiting through the slightly ajar window next to my head and making for Stragill shore at Lough Swilly to watch the gentle waves lapping on the orange rippled strand before moving on.

Mid way through the third decade of the Rosary, a black-haired boy with red cheeks and well-fed face appeared at the window next to me. He summoned John outside with a silent but furious wave through the white lace curtains, eyes pleading with him as the sky fell in around his shoulders. He had a panicked look, as if he was going to end up in the next grave along to me. John bumped silently through the mourners kneeling at chairs, as Rosary beads jangled in clasped hands to allow the boy through. They reached the front wall of the house leading down the lane at the same time.

"What's the matter Cormac? Why the wild rush?" John asked his mate.

"Fifteen head of cattle have escaped from the Ballynarry fields while the old fella is in the town. He asked me to fix the gap with whun bushes and barbed wire this morning and, well, well, I forgot didn't I. He'll kill me surely this time", Cormac replied breathless, his heart pounding in panic and fear.

"Come on then, we'll find them and get them in before he gets back from the town, he'll be none the wiser if we go now before dark", John replied. He picked up two blackthorn sticks that I had left behind the wall for this type of thing and the two boys made off down my long, steep laneway towards the Lough. If the cattle were still on the road, there was half a chance of getting them back in before nightfall. If they were in another farmer's field already, maybe tramping through freshly sown corn or potatoes, then it was going to be a long night, and enemies were made in rural areas for a lot less. John knew that at least Pat Gavin was out of the picture and wouldn't be shifted until tomorrow morning if the tea and sandwiches and smokes kept rolling. Nothing like other people's smokes to give Pat the craving for nicotine, not to mention a house full of buxom women missing top buttons serving food into the wee hours, it was enough to make the old bachelor's nose run and eyes water from pure joy.

The boys checked over every ditch between Keelogs and Stragill shore, as well as in the clearing leading to the rippled orange strand, but the cattle were nowhere to be seen. They made their way back up towards Ballynarry again and this time went down the lower road, taking in the Planting, where the road was covered in a canopy of birch, oak and hazelnut trees and had been there for a million years before today. The forest floor was dense with mushrooms and bluebells and moss that hadn't seen the light of day for two hundred years and edged sharply into the dark water of the river coming from the Backhill. Black stones, glossy under the water and green moss above made the purest clear water gargle and come alive from the depths of the earth. Black eels hid, dark as night, under the moist soft ledges where branches snared by the last flood provided a wicker roof to their private world.

Cormac spotted the cattle down by the river and began counting them. For the love of Jesus, Mary and Joseph, they were all there and accounted for, even the rhony heifer with the mad stare and the young bullock that nearly died from pneumonia before Christmas. They were surprisingly well settled after their dash for freedom and grazed on the sweet new grass in the wild Irish forest. They stomped through the undergrowth; the sound of their fat noses bellowing was drowned out by the crackling of their hooves through the fallen branches. With the gentle persuasion and experience of men twice their age, the boys moved the cattle slowly along the river's edge to the small opening by the stone bridge. If they got them out single file, nice and ginger like, it was a short herd along the busy road to Ballynarry. Calmness was the way to walking any beast on the road. I taught John that and I didn't think he was listening at the time, not until I grabbed his arm and squeezed it to make sure the information was getting through. I had a grip like no other man and, back then, the grip was my way of communicating to young fellas.

The Planting was a special place, a place of reverence for all things natural. Ghost stories were told of its great loneliness, walking through her bosom on the darkest nights in the dead of winter; love songs were written of its warm summer days and balmy evenings, warm blankets and love making on her rustic floor. Her new life affected the whole of Donegal in springtime. Foxes howled on the far side of the river, warding off intruders, while children, unaware of the need to be scared, picked hazelnuts in brown ripened clusters at harvest. Fairies and nature sprites lived here in harmony with everything else, protecting the place, stewards of the earth and protectors of traditions. Badgers and foxes lived side by side, raising their young in deep lairs, left alone by the world around them.

The boys steered the fifteen head of cows, heifers and bullocks to the narrow opening as if they were a friendly presence behind the group. If one startled or took a notion, they could split in opposite directions. Separated from the rest, they were likely to end up on the Buncrana Road, where a chance meeting with Cormac's father after six hours in Flaherty's pub, staggering, fierce, strong and cross, was a sure-fire death sentence for all involved, John Devenney included.

Chapter 2

Dinny Hegarty nodded silently for another round. He normally didn't spend time down this way and was glad of the anonymity, for a hundred different reasons. Mulligan's pub was as far away from Derry City as any place could be, not by miles travelled but a completely slower pace. There were no questions asked here, or guilt implied, and there was no judgement either way. Blending in here was easier said than done with his accent. He tried it with the farmers after Mass, lamenting potato prices and the late frost th'year delaying the cutting of the turf. The Dublin registration on his blue Mark III Cortina parked outside and Dinny's Derry accent meant that no questions would be asked. A nod was as good as a wink at Mulligan's, where strangers were either on their way from bother or heading towards it.

Mulligan's pub didn't open every day; it depended solely on how Peter woke up that morning. Toss of a coin to open or close. If the locals saw the white smoke from the chimney in the front lounge, it was open. They called it the Sistine chapel of Inishowen and Peter the Holy Father of the Parish. It was Saint Patrick's Day on Tuesday and men were getting thirsty in anticipation of breaking Lent for the day, so the Holy Father lit the fire, and the Papal signal went out. The pub was whitewashed and had small opaque windows for a bit of privacy while you drank. The front door led straight onto the Linsfort road, directly onto the path of oncoming traffic, which would be a problem except there was little traffic on the road apart from local farmers, an odd tourist and men like Dinny — on the run. Although Peter was an awkward character and you either loved or hated him, he was trusted by the Derry brigade and his black wall phone was one of the most secure lines in the Republic of Ireland.

A French tourist entered the bar, with no regard for Northern or Republican registrations, frustrated at being lost and directed the wrong way four times by locals saying, "just go straight on". He punched his French finger through the ten times folded map as he asked Peter a third time in broken English for the Gap of Mamore. "Is this way, no?" he asked again. Peter lifted his heavy stomach off the bar and rubbed his well shaven chin, his deadpan eyes sat lazily in their sockets and looked like they could have done with at least three hours more sleep. He pointed out the door and the French man's eyes followed.

"Go out here, turn left and then keep going until ye hit the fort in front of ye, then turn right at the stone bridge and Mamore Gap will be there to greet ye. It's the steep road between the two mountains. Watch the sheep now, they lay in the middle of the road for the heat", he laughed and the men with red faces from drink and windswept weather looked up and laughed with him.

"Have a drink before ye go sure and take your woman in too", Peter waved her in with the almost white cloth that had been on his shoulder. She leaned over and stretched her seatbelt across her ample breasts and spoke in a dainty French accent. "Il est beaucoup trop tôt pour boire un verre dans un pub irlandais, il faut y aller André" ("It's much too early for a drink in an Irish pub, we must go Andre"), her blond hair fell on the steering wheel. It was the wrong side of the road for Ireland, but right in every other way.

Dinny caught her eye, and she smiled across the language barrier, another time, another place. He imagined her Parisian lifestyle, meeting her for breakfast, and as the car pulled away with Andre still sporting a vexed head and narrow shoulders, in his mind's eye he had met her long before breakfast, with no Andre in sight.

Dinny wished that life could be this simple. He lit a cigarette, took a deep drag that calmed his nerves and sank deeper into the warm seat under the window. The fire belted out heat from the open fireplace and the room had an aroma of heather, peat and clear air that could only be smelt by unfamiliar strangers from Derry and tourists from France and America.

At 3.30 sharp, the phone rang in the room behind the bar. Dinny got up to answer it. Everyone else ignored the sound and The Holy Father stepped from behind the bar to stoke the fire and put on more turf. Dinny crouched his athletic body on the worn black stool and pressed his dark moustache against the receiver, saying little, listening intently. His heart sank as he was instructed to stay in Donegal indefinitely as his mugshot was on display at every British Army and RUC checkpoint from Coshquin to Aughnacloy. He placed the phone back down and sat quietly, in stunned silence, looking out at the Lough. Its tranquillity made him feel like rowing a small boat to the centre by the red buoy and jumping into the darkness, joining the crew of the Laurentic ship laying on the ocean floor with all her lost gold, cold, useless, worthless and dead.

Time had gotten away from Dinny and what started as a pint to wait on the call, ended up five deep as the grey clouds rolled across Inishowen. Lights started appearing in farmhouses along the Hillside. It was time to go. He checked his pockets for smokes and the keys jangled in his jacket pocket. He stepped out onto the Parish Road and was greeted by a squally March shower that battered hailstones on his blue Cortina. The tape was already in the cassette player and, as the engine fired up on the dark blue Mark III, Big Tom took up where he left off four hours ago.

"Four roads to Glenamaddy, four roads that drift apart, four roads to Glenamaddy, and four dusty highways to my heart".

Dinny loved all things country music and, like everybody else in Inishowen, loved Big Tom McBride. He sat for a while, idling the engine with the choke pulled out, letting the engine warm up, hopeful of warm air from the blower. The wipers screeched across the cold windscreen, clearing the white pellets of icy hail and rain from his line of vision. He checked his mirrors and surroundings. Something wasn't right. There was a feeling, and he'd learned to trust these feelings because they had kept him alive until now. He reversed the car around to the back street and left the engine running. He slipped out quietly, clicking the door gently behind him. Laying in the grassy ditch, he had a good view of the main road and could see a hundred metres either way. The cold and wet from the long grass and bare hawthorn bushes seeped through his large frame but he lay silently, breathing only when necessary, looking in on his own scene with the eye of a hawk, or a trained military man.

Almost five minutes had passed when a green Vauxhall Cavalier with two men inside drove slowly past the pub towards the fort. To the casual observer, they paid little attention to the idling Cortina, but they had no business down this way on a Sunday afternoon. They weren't local or lost tourists, and they certainly weren't on their way to see men about potato gathering or the price of sheep dip. Dinny's gut had served him well again although he damned his own actions earlier for having one too many. He began to map the way to the safe house in his head. It would be a fast run back by the side roads — he needed to stay off the main road on a Sunday afternoon, where Guards might be pulling or have checkpoints set up. The Irish guards would be the least of his worries, if the pair in the Cavalier were on a mission from the Crown forces, he might not see the day out.

Crouching like a man under helicopter blades, he made a beeline for the idling Cortina and screeched off the street, spitting gravel onto the low white-washed wall. The Holy Father stepped into the kitchen and dialled the Northern number on the black wall phone. The man answered, "Yes?"

Peter pulled at the black concertinaed wire leading to the receiver and replied, "He's on the move".

The line went dead.

Chapter 3

The Druid Queen lay peacefully under a dolmen in a sheltered small field, out of sight and happy to be so. A gentle blackthorn fairy tree grew alongside her. From her vantage point, with a view of Stragill shore, Lough Swilly and the Atlantic beyond, the Queen saw everything, and she certainly heard John and Cormac walking up the Planting. She smiled at their innocence and felt the calmness of the evening. Although she had rested there for near on five thousand years, I was beginning to realise that it was less than an hour in our time. She promised life protection for these boys because they were pure Donegal, nothing more and nothing less, with not a hint of outside influence. They belonged to the land of TirConnell and were as much a part of it as the water in the river and the stones that lay within it. She stayed alert now. A scene was set, and she readied her magical powers.

The light was fading as the cows were masterfully herded onto the road leading to Ballynarry. The leading cow sniffed at the grass on the verge and emptied her back end onto the middle of the road. Cormac was out front, waving his blackthorn stick, while John was ten metres behind them, goading them forward slowly and calmly. There was only a hundred metres to go until the cattle would be in before dark and not a word would be said about it. There was a quietness as they walked in unison, and it was the first time that John had been left alone with his own thoughts since I had passed. We were very close. He was the only young fella that would speak loud enough for me to hear and, more importantly, he was the only one I wanted to hear, despite the angst of my wife and the pain that it invoked.

"Turn that hearing aid up George, for Christ's sake, John has me deafened and ye can hear him in Burnfoot", my wife roared constantly, lighting another cigarette to go with the last twenty, arm on the range, coughing by the fire.

-

Dinny had no choice but stay on the main road out of the Parish until he got to the top of Claggan Road that led down to Stragill shore. The road was narrow with wild grass growing in the centre and straggly blackberry briars and green nettles on the sides. Trails of muck added to the slippery brae where milking cows crossed morning and night. Dinny knew the roads here well and the speed that they could be driven at. He reefed a hard right on the steering wheel. The back end of the Cortina sprayed gravel onto the bare hazelnut trees from the loose stones at the intersection. As he looked to the right, the nose of the green Cavalier was rounding the corner on the main road at full speed. He took off down Claggan Road as the grass in the centre lapped against the front grill. The Cavalier did a handbrake turn too, no more than ten seconds later, and followed him with the skill of a man that had done it before.

The Cortina was airborne as Dinny came around the sharp bend. The width of the road was barely enough for one car, and he sank the boot fully to the floor. There wasn't time to look in the mirrors but the definite roar of an engine behind him meant they weren't far away. He slowed slightly at the crossroads and pulled hard on the handbrake again before planting the accelerator to the floor. Everything shook. The glovebox opened and the revolver dropped down onto the passenger footwell. It would be needed if he didn't get away. The vibrations from the car jump started the tape, and as four country roads rang out, he quickly went through the gears up the Planting Road. The car smelt of burnt oil and hot wiring. The oil light came on and the temperature gauge was well into the red. The tyres sizzled in the cool evening. The car behind gained ground as the roar of the engines got louder. The Planting became an amphitheatre of sound like a time trial for the Donegal rally.

-

A cow doctor named Dan Dotton walked with a steady pace up the Planting road. He stepped in time with his freshly cut birch stick, click, click, clicking on the tarmac. Dan had qualifications from the potato field university like most local men but had spent five years on the rounds with a respected veterinarian surgeon from Burnfoot. Dan was the poor man's vet; he was paid in tea, eggs, fry ups, sweet afton smokes and scone bread. He knew every animal in the Parish and visited every family, including my own, where he drank tea and read tea leaves and talked of a united Ireland.

He was on his way to my wake with a good pace. His smoke glowed bright red, held in place by sucked-in, toothless lips being fanned by his speed; he could already feel the heat of the kitchen and taste the warm sugary tea. His yellow three-quarter trench coat was black and shiny at the pockets and collar from years of travel. He jumped onto the mossy bank as the cars roared up the Planting and screeched at the crossroads. He slipped, falling backwards onto the forest floor, covering the back of his best yellow coat in dirt and muck. His going out shoes were mucky and wet.

Dan waved the six-foot stick at the noisy bastards and memorised their Derry and Dublin plates. A number plate in Inishowen was like stripes to an American soldier, and it determined how the occupant could and should be saluted. Local people and Donegal plates, big smile, full Donegal wave salute and a guaranteed wave back. Derry plates, be wary, a lukewarm smile and may or may not salute with only a fair to middling chance of their waving back. Dublin plates could be Gardai, Special Branch or an obnoxious tourist from the capital, run them off the road, no smile, no salute — Dan couldn't give a fiddler's fuck if they waved back or not.

"Go away home to fuck, bastards to hell youse, no respect there rallying and a wake not a quarter mile as the crow flies", Dan called after both cars. He couldn't help thinking he'd seen the Dublin Cortina earlier that day. He blessed himself. Looking to the Heavens, he prayed silently on an inward whisper that the noise wouldn't be heard at my house and disrupt the Rosary. He didn't know that I was standing beside him, but he sensed me, and he shivered like he'd brushed against an electric fence. He took a moment to straighten himself up as the noise of the cars suddenly disappeared and got himself settled for the sanctity and reverence needed to greet my mourning family. He wiped himself down and lit another smoke.

-

John was deep in thought and wiped a tear from his eye, knowing our chats in the evening time were over. He needed his grandfather to make sense of life and he had more complications than most. He often talked out loud on this road and it was as though the Planting itself was listening, caring and somehow making things right. The cows were past the fork in the road and Cormac was already at the ramshackle gate. Although there was still enough light to see what was in front of him, it was too dark to read the black face of his watch. John strained to see the time and dropped the stick in the middle of the road, bending down and holding his wrist with the other hand to get a better look. He lifted his head in the split second. There was a mighty roar of an engine and then nothing. The sky came and went in a blur as the blue flash revved under him. Sharp pain, warm and electric, shot across his body. He watched himself flying through the air in slow motion, an eternity of time passing by. His black shoes, loosely laced and muddy, flew in opposite directions, one making a splash in the river and the other lost forever in the hawthorn hedge. He felt calm, almost protected from the moment, like it was happening to someone else, and he was sat there watching it in the Buncrana cinema. There was loud, thunderous noise everywhere, but inside his head there was only silence.

Within seconds, the mayhem was over but for the muffled sound of another car in the distance. John was face down in a puddle of muck, next to the river. He lay there motionless, heart beating but unable to breathe. Blood began to seep from his right ear. The five-centimetre cut above his right eye didn't have a chance to bleed yet in the mucky faceplant. There was nothing I could do but watch my grandson die before me, well ahead of his time. I called for Cormac's help, but of course no one heard me. It was the divine order of things, and I had to accept it. I waited an eternity in those seconds asking why I should suffer the pain of seeing this, and whether it was definitely his time. The answer came.

The planting came alive.

Small hands, many small hands, carefully turned John on his side. He groaned as gargled air hissed from his chest and, immediately after, he took a deep breath and filled his lungs, coughing and spluttering, a stream of blood, water and muck spewing onto the green grass. They lifted his limp arms, bruised and bent from the impact. The perfect shape of my thin grandson was heavily impressed in the watery ground as he was carried under the barren birch tree and sat upright. Had I been alive and full of prejudice and thick irreverence, I would have said my eyes were deceiving me, but the world I knew nothing of until two days ago was the only world I knew now. I would have thanked them but either they couldn't see me or chose not to.

The Druid Queen appeared dressed in a white robe, almost translucent in appearance, wearing a necklace of green and blue gemstones. Her hair was blond, almost white, tied behind her back and her eyes were bright emerald under dark eyebrows. I had never encountered a more beautiful woman; I don't think words in the English language exist to describe her properly. She held her arms aloft, bringing life and energy back to John as the area around him buzzed with life. She spoke in Gaelic and chanted to the heavens as the whites of her eyes rolled back in her head.

"Go dtuga Dia na talún, na gaoithe, na tine agus an éitear an leanbh íon seo dÉirinn ar ais ar a chosán ceart, Mar sin, bíodh sé" ("May the God of earth, wind, fire and ether return this pure child of Eireann to his rightful path, so be it")

The small helpers, twelve in total, watched for a time and formed a ring of light around John, then transcended the darkness, pulling life from everywhere into a single point of love. They left in four directions, leaving John and the Queen alone. She sensed my presence and spoke to me without words. I thanked her for intervening from my newfound state. Finally, she kissed his forehead and the light from her eyes burnt bright into his before she disappeared into the darkness.

-

Ian Douglas and Mark May kept off the main roads as much as possible. They were supposed to observe only, watch, and if the opportunity arose, apprehend Dinny and bring him back to Fort George. It would have been a great day's work. Both British intelligence agents had children of their own and although every Paddy was a target when it came to counter terrorism, with the almost sure death of the young boy that they witnessed earlier, there was going to be questions asked in Derry tonight and their stories had to match.

"Turn left here, and slowly", Ian instructed Mark, as the tension of the chase gave way to a calm sense of 'nothing to see here'. They were trained for this, to kill without emotion under exoneration of doing it for Queen and country, but leaving a child to die was not only a blight on their target, it was also a blight on themselves. Neither man spoke until they were well on the Derry side of Buncrana, and they radioed ahead to the Coshquin border for a silent entry. Two tall Mayo Guards sat in their inconspicuous special branch car and noted the passing of their British counterparts through Fahan. They photographed Ian and Mark, stoney faced and pale like they'd been duelling with the devil and lived to tell the tale, driving calmly back to Northern Ireland with no one in the back seat and a seemingly light and empty boot.

"We should be charging them for taking that much Donegal soil back to Derry. There's enough on the side of that car to form another island to fight for, I tell you, what", Tom O'Malley scratched at his black moustache and laughed. The elbow of his obligatory black leather jacket squeaked against the car door.

"There's something going on here Mick, I tell you that. Our friends have been rallying or chasing or both. Let's see if the Holy Father has anything to say for himself, what", Tom indicated the direction of Dunree fort with a large, white, soft hand in flat palm, not point, military style gesture for his partner Mick O'Dowd, also known as Ass's Teeth, to have a drive down to the Parish and see if there was a story to be told. It was like getting blood from a stone for the most part, but worth a try. Any chance to put his size thirteen on Peter Mulligan's throat was a good day at the office for Tom. Popularity prizes were hard to come by around here and asking after men on the run, Special Branch or not, could be your last question asked.

Ass's Teeth yawned like a neighing donkey as they drove towards Buncrana and the reason for his nickname became apparent: his set of gnashers were tea stained, gnarly and strong as whitewashed pillars.

"Let's see if the Holy Father has been performing the last rites at his latest lock in." Mick had to stop himself from adding a 'what' to the end of his sentence — spending all day in the car with Tommy was rubbing off on him. "Another run to the ass end of the world, ass end of Europe, ass end of Donegal and the ass end of the Parish, what?" Mick roared with laughter and to hell with poverty, he'd say what as often as Tommy now and sprayed his laughter onto the steering wheel of the Mark V Cortina. It was obvious to Tom that he'd never heard his own donkey's ass nickname.

"If the Holy father is bound by the confessional, then the wee Altar Boy will know". Mick pulled the notepad from his top pocket and threw it on the dash in anticipation. He didn't mention they would see Tadhg Byrne. Tom brushed a hair from the arm of his jacket. Even between themselves, they rarely mentioned his real name.

Chapter 4

"Holy jumpin' Jesus, what happened you?" Paddy Ennis, the poteen maker, asked Dinny as he stepped away from the still in the middle of the Augaweel forestry.

"You look like you've seen a ghost", he shook his head and walked around the car three times, kicking the hot tyres and inspecting the dent on the front, the broken windscreen and the muck from asshole to breakfast time with his torch light.

"Honestly Paddy, I think I hit a cow down by the Planting being chased by the boys", Dinny replied, shaking, his hands wouldn't stop shaking since leaving Mulligan's.

"How did they know or was it just bad timing?" he asked, face buried in his hands as they went inside the brewers' hut, miles from anywhere and the safest place in Ireland. Dinny's heart began to settle and as the effects of the afternoon pints lifted, a feeling of overwhelming panic and guilt came over him. Paddy went back to bottling poteen and occasionally glanced at Dinny. Full facial and eye contact would have given his true thoughts away. Paddy had piercing bright green eyes, mad eyes, Celtic through and through and regardless of Dinny's lips moving, he had the ability to look into his soul and see what actually happened. For a second, he felt the panic and fear and saw the scene. He brushed his scraggly shoulder length hair to the back of his head and held his rough brown beard in his hands. This was no ordinary car chase.

Dinny had looked back at his pursuers when he got to the Planting crossroads. It seemed like a split second, maybe more than that, maybe it was ten seconds — he couldn't really piece it together — but he heard the thud on the bonnet, breaking glass and cows scattering off onto the side of the road. He lost them and they stopped the pursuit then and there. A dead cow could be compensated for but being caught didn't bear thinking about; twenty years in the

Maze prison was the least of his worries if he even made it that far. Unlimited interrogation and helicopter flights for volunteers was part of the mind games played.

"What if it wasn't a cow? It could have been anyone, I have no way of knowing unless we go back there now and see how the land lies." Dinny was panicked now, the unknowing, the what if, maybe, can't be sure, drove him demented and he rocked over and back on the brewer's chair, arms folded, crouched, like a lunatic in an asylum, tortured by himself.

"We'll go back there tomorrow, Dinny. We'll speak to a few of the farmers, whatever damage has been done will be paid for with no questions asked, now give me a hand to cover this car." Paddy tried to settle his nerves and pulled the heavy green tarpaulin over the car and cut fresh pine branches to cover it completely. He thought about torching it tonight, but it would get too much attention, and he felt sure they were already looking for it. From where he was standing, it was a person and no cow that he'd hit. Asking questions to anyone was an admission of guilt. He knew the funeral was on tomorrow and all the locals would be there, Pat Gavin, Dan Dotton and anyone who was anyone would be lamenting. The social event at Cockhill Chapel was a day out with friends. It was a funeral on him anyway and we were cousins in some one way or another. He bottled the last of the batch and left Dinny in the hut, warning him to stay put until tomorrow evening. He walked back over the hill with an empty gas bottle to sleep in the home house. He'd wash at the basin in the morning, sleeves up, collar down, wash what ye can see. It was a day for the black suit and to farewell old George, to farewell me.

The late March wind got up over the mountains and blew in from the North Atlantic. The tops of the pine trees swayed in unison but below, at the makeshift hut with four trees as corner posts, Dinny slept intermittently by the red-hot turf fire. His eyes moved rapidly as he finally drifted off. Reality and dreaming became one, and suddenly everything was real. I was in it, John, Dan Dotton, the works. Every soul he'd ever known, helped, hindered, hated or killed was there. All meant to be. Coincidences a human construct in the game of life as contracts were signed, sealed and delivered long before meeting on the earthly plain. The name John Devenney came to him as he fell off the kerb, into a trance-like sleep. The boy of fourteen smiled at him, thanking him for their brief meeting and the reason that he was now reunited with his Druid ancestors. All things were linked and meant to be, karma added, subtracted, grace banks emptied and filled, life lived. He slept soundly until the slow and silent appearance of Monday morning under the cover of the pine trees, a grey day, a rolling grey cloud day, March 22nd 1981, the day of my funeral.

Chapter 5

Cormac herded the last of the fifteen cattle into the field. Their heavy hooves stammered and stomped in the slippery muck almost a foot deep. They ran into the field like possessed devils.

"Easy on there John, there's no need to batter them at the gap", he called to John but couldn't hear himself speak. He listened to Hotel California in full on the Sony Walkman he had stolen from his sister and the Eagles tape from under his brother's pillow. There would be a battering for it, but some things were worth it when he thought of all the other pain he endured for absolutely no gain. The electric guitar at the end was his favourite and he turned the volume up fully. Never had sound penetrated his ears like this, walking around like this, no one else listening — just pure pleasure and the cattle back in, and no one the wiser. He played air guitar and thought how rich these boys must be, lighting fires with ten-pound notes and a woman for every night of the week.

He pulled the six strands of barbed wire taut and put the base of the last post into the round stirrup at the bottom of the stay post and another loop at the top. He let go and the wire dropped on the ground like a spineless man trying to stand up after a day in Flaherty's. He started propping the intermediate posts while he waited for John, thinking he may have taken off to get back to the wake. John being his best friend in not just words, he preferred actions and today's help released his head from a noose that would never be forgotten, no matter how many corners they turned in life or how old they lived, it was set in stone.

John sat up and propped his thin frame against the wall of the stone bridge, legs pointing towards the middle of the road. He felt calm, warm, almost floating and still had the feeling of looking at the world through someone else's eyes. It was just on dark now. The Planting trees and bushes appeared like black silhouettes against the last gasp of faded light. His left eye was warm and damp, and blood trickled down the side of his face. He held the back of his hand to the two-inch tear on his eyebrow. He got to his feet and looking down at his holey black sodden socks, realised his shoes were gone and his heart sank. His shoulders twitched, and his scalp buzzed like a thousand midges had descended on top of his head and danced in unison. Was this real? Déjà vu took hold. The recurring dream about losing one shoe or both, being chased barefoot back to Keelogs and the search, the unending search, for those missing shoes. Suddenly the wild bother he was in dissipated. It didn't matter now. He felt the soft grass beneath his feet, finally grounded. The Druid Queen and fairies were nowhere to be seen, but he felt their presence. He would feel their presence until his last day in the potato field. They would never leave his side. My grandson was now one-part Devenney, one-part Doherty, Celtic, Fairy, wholly Druid and fully Irish.

-

The front bar at Mulligan's was full. Regulars' chairs with their names on were occupied and Peter's wife served a steady string of Guinness and wee half's. It was a better Sunday evening than most when word got around that the bar was open all day. Tommy and Mick entered through the front door and ducked their heads walking over the threshold. They stood out like foxes in a henhouse, like Mayo men in a Donegal pub, like gardai in Mulligan's, plain clothes or not. There was a silent nod from one of the locals. The news was on in a small timber boxed television at the end of the bar and it blared softly in muffled tones of the hunger strike and mounting tension. No one listened, not intentionally anyway.

The pub went silent.

"Boss about, what?" Tom asked Brigid Mary behind the bar.

"Hold on Tom, I'll get him now. Do you want a drink while you're standin' there?" She rubbed her nose with the back of her hand and topped up three pints of Guinness.

"No, we're fine now, what, just a word now and we'll be on our way."

Tom spoke with authority, clear, concise and with the backing of the badge. His dark black hair was brushed back and he would have interest from any woman in the Parish, if there was any there. Brigid Mary cast a second glance as she finished the pints and he smiled, his blue eyes followed her movements, patient, warm and calm. He was a brave man and played his part well. It wasn't for everyone. He felt like an intruder, and he was an intruder. Ass's Teeth stood behind him like a mule on donkey derby day, waiting at the starting line, his tail twisted by the farmer and salt on his arse to move him. The back door would have been much more personable, less intrusive, but the front door showed everyone, especially Peter, that they were onto him, by how much was for them to know and Peter to find out.

"Guards, please, follow me." Peter came from behind the bar and directed them into the small kitchen. "What would you like to discuss?"

He sat at the small table and gestured they sit but both men stood, their six foot plus frames towering over him.

"Looking for men that may have been rallying through the Parish today, getting reports of disturbances, ye wouldn't have seen or heard anything, what?" Tom asked the question with no hope of a reply.

"It's been a quiet day officers, the day was in it and big George's funeral tomorrow, the whole of the Parish is in mourning — he was well thought of. But no, saw nothing other than a couple of French tourists looking for Mamore gap if that's any good to you."

"Peter, can we have a straight conversation.? If there are foreign forces operating in your neck of the woods, then it benefits you and us to know what's going on. If you help us, we can help you, what."

The Holy Father looked up at the guards with his right hand against his temple, thinking, remembering, in total reflection.

"I have no errand against any man, friend or foe, it's none of my business what happens, and I see next to nothing down in this backwater anyway, but if I see anything or hear of anything like that, you will both be the first to know." Peter got to his feet, standing eye to eye with his visitors and showed them his palm-not-point hand gesture towards the back door. The talk was over. Go in peace.

"He knows, Tom. He knows what's going on, I tell you that now", Mick said as they drove off, the 'what' a whisper under his breath.

"Of course, he knows Mick, of course he does", Tom replied and let out a long, drawn-out thinking 'what' that he didn't even realise he'd said. Next stop was to see the wee Altar Boy.

Chapter 6

Most of the family sat up all night at my wake. Old customs die hard in the Northwest. A constant run of tea and tins of biscuits, pastries from Lynch's bakery, smokes from Brendan Craig's grocery van and sandwiches kept them going until the early hours. Cars were parked on both sides of the road at the bottom of my steep lane, although it wasn't my lane anymore. The walls of the farmhouse were freshly whitewashed and the uneven walls looked regal, even if I say so myself. The byre and barn doors, painted red also, were barrel bolted shut, the sight of loose straw and cow dung out of sight and out of mind. The street was scuffled for unsightly grass and a load of new stones spread on the first morning of the wake made a welcome crunch under the mourners' feet. The Bangor slates on the roof were old, weathered, and crooked in parts, but somehow regal in a townland known for thatch, small windows and poverty. The outside dry toilet, around the side of the house, had its black bucket emptied regularly and Jayes Fluid to keep it fresh. A proper, homely, Donegal wake, even if I say so myself.

My father Con was a blacksmith of some repute and made more money in the forge on the other side of the road than ten drinking men could spend in a lifetime. It seemed like a lifetime since he lay where I am now, on a white sheet on the dead bed, black crucifixes pinned around the outside. I never thought the day would come for me, but I suppose it arrives for everyone eventually, and although it was more than forty-five years ago, it feels like the blink of an eye; where I am, there's neither yesterday, today nor tomorrow, only now.

The sun rose slowly. Light came from nowhere, silently, softly, without any warmth, but eventually it brightened enough, and the outside light went off. John stood outside my window, his black eye swollen, multiple stitches with black needle and thread, numbed by a frozen fish finger, from Cormac the poor man's surgeon general late last night. For what he'd been through and what I saw thanks to the Queen, he was glad to be upright, walking. He was glad to be alive.

John glanced down at his shoes. His feet were cold in someone else's plimsolls, half a size too small, the cold stones from the street penetrating through the soles like he was standing on ice bricks. Somewhere in the great city of Glasgow, there was another boy, probably slightly older, that first wore the plimsolls and every other article of clothing that John possessed, apart from clothes bought from the potato field economy. When the tread on the plimsolls was eighty per cent depleted or the boy grew out of them, whichever came first, then they, along with every other conceivable garment for boy, girl, adult or child, summer or winter, old stock, unsellable or jumble sale, was sent to Keelogs in a brown paper parcel, tied up with string — cheap mail, and the Broons comic strip from the newspaper. Josies parcel. Everyone seemed to have relations in either Glasgow or Liverpool, and John's mother still considered Josie, her friend from the orphanage as her best friend and sister. The shoes were once black, but grey and faded now and in another time and place they may have even looked alright. He had sat the shoes under the sideboard before going to bed and polished them with lashings of black boot polish, enough to fill the holes and scrapes on the toes, enough to turn his second-hand Scotch runners into grandfather funeral shoes, hoping no one would notice. He placed one foot over the other to hide them and didn't look at anyone's face as they gathered at the house, but looked at their feet first, the style of them, the polish on them, the cow dung on them, the squeak of real leather or the squelch of plastic, warmth, comfort, style, rich and poor, scuffed and pristine. He could tell a lot about a person by the shoes they wore; I taught him that.

I stood there with Cormac, John and his youngest brother, Liam, and watched them intently as my final journey from Keelogs to Cockhill Chapel was about to commence. John held Liam's hand. The boy struggled to get away, wriggling his thin white fingers out of John's grip.

"Let me go, let me go John, ya shite. I want to go in and see Granda", he protested loudly and punched his brother in the ribs.

"Stay with me out here and I'll buy you a choc ice after the funeral", John replied, "but only if you behave yourself and quit the carry on here and now."

Men in well-to-do black suits and nice shoes looked down their noses at my grandsons. Their eyes said that a bit of manners wouldn't go astray, and that it looked like the bigger one had already fought the first two rounds and lost them both. Don Macklin, standing thin and bandy-legged, leaned back to whisper in his wife's ear, but with the sound of silence and his own deafness, his words carried clearly across the forty mourners on the street. "Fucken talking when he should have been listening, they're all the same them boys, and never will be no good for nothing except gathering perdies and footing turf", he smiled condescendingly at the cut of them. His wife, who had eaten all of the breakfasts that Don had no time or inclination to eat, shushed him to be quiet. People coughed and moved away like the parting of the black sea in a middle eastern parable.

Paddy Poteen had his back to the low whitewashed wall on the street. He threw his smoke onto the gravel and made a deliberate loud stomp to butt it out. The smoke was well and truly extinguished, and Don Macklin looked back to catch his eye. Nothing annoyed Paddy more than thran, hateful old bastards giving young fellas a hard time or making them feel as low as their circumstances dictated. He knew the youngest boy was disabled, how much, he wasn't sure, but one thing was for sure, those weans didn't have a pot to pish in, metaphorically or physically. Their story echoed his own and most of the people on the street that morning, whether they cared to admit it or not. Paddy's bright green eyes widened with a slow-released rage, but now was neither the time nor the place, besides, he couldn't make a scene as the Altar Boy, Tadhg Byrne, was standing close by and whatever was said within earshot of him went straight back to the Garda Siochana. With one of the North's most wanted men at the poteen den, and his own colourful relationship with the Guards, every word was a clue, every sentence a contract and the Altar Boy could smell a good story better than any journalist.

John watched Paddy from a distance, he admired the man, his legendary run-ins with the Guards, his care factor and disdain for farming and clergy and, mostly, his success in the face of futility and mediocrity. Paddy, on the other hand, eyed the young fella up and the penny dropped. He'd talk to him when the time was right. It was no right hook that caused his closed eye.

The mood was sombre. Loud cries of grief and muffled sobs from family and neighbours could be heard in the otherwise quiet house. John looked in through the white lace curtain and bid me farewell as the lid went on. Liam picked up a white stone from amongst the new gravel and licked it. Don shook his head and nudged his wife that was now standing three feet from him. Pale patches of lime from the whitewashed wall had turned Liam's shiny blue trouser into a painter's uniform. Dan Dotton ducked his head at the door and walked out in front of me. I followed him onto the street with my physical body following behind, being carried, bumping doorways, dead, lifeless and cold. Pat Gavin and Dan stood to the right of the front door, just off the step. Between them, looking up at them, stood Tadhg, all four foot eight of him. His pointy eyes were black and deadened, his hair shaved around his puny, pointy head, like an American GI. His ears stood out like cold trumpets, red, listening and foundered. He was not well known in my house but people from the Parish were within their rights to turn up on account of this one or on account of that one, and, in Tadhg's mind, he turned up on account of gathering information, being nosey generally and most of all to fulfill his mission — to find out why the big rush for the British Intelligence to leave the Parish last night.

A feeling of great satisfaction came over him as he huddled between the two men most likely to know the craic and he pulled the lapels of his would-be special branch Crombie around his ears. It was almost a two mile walk to Cockhill and there would be plenty of time for questions that weren't questions, but conversation, information gathering conversation. The wind started up from the shore. An early morning wind that carried squally showers at forty-five degrees from Rathmullan. There was no druth to dry clothes or turf in the hill. It was a hard, cold, biting and wet squall for the mourners; I felt nothing.

The rain was on as I got the first lift to the bottom of the lane. Angels cried and a poor dog in the distance, distraught, foundered and tied to a plough with only a cloth bag for bedding, wailed and lamented, adding to the final act of theatre. The half door was open in the forge as I was carried past. The familiar sound of the horseshoe being shaped on the anvil warmed my heart. I looked around to see if anyone else could hear it. Everyone carried on walking, slow-paced except John and me. We walked over, even though the path was now overgrown with rushes and blackberry bushes and we leaned on the smithy's door. The sparks bounced across the floor, red, hot and bright to the eye. The horse, Hughie, stood silently and ate from his nose bag. He was a good horse, a great worker on the plough, but, like me, was a thran enough bastard from way back. He turned around and noticed us at the door, all of us on the wrong side of the knackers except John — who was alive in both worlds. My father stood up with a red-hot horseshoe in the tongs and saw us. His eyes lit up from the warmth of the forge fire. He held up Hughie's front hoof and imprinted the shoe, hot and smoky. He watched us intently, without breaking stride from the job at hand. Tears of joy fell off his youthful face. it was the first time I had seen him cry. He held the hot shoe in the black bucket. The water hissed and the steam rose into his face as it cooled. As it cleared, my mother, Midge, young and beautiful, stood beside him.

They nodded silently and welcomed me, their only son, into the land of the living, with an embrace that, once again I have not the English capacity to explain, only to say that the pure love I felt at that moment was worth every day I had spent here. They acknowledged John with the same embrace. The events of yesterday, every part of it, every player in it, the unfolding of the story to the most minute detail, was more scripted than an Oscar-winning film. I knew this forge so well, every stone, every tool, every memory. The stool that I sat on as a boy, just inside the door and distance enough away from the kick from a horse, sat in its spot, empty. I wondered if it was an invitation to sit for a while and I looked at John as if he had the answer. When I looked back, my eldest son, Con, appeared, silently at first, as if he had just woken from a deep sleep or was in two places at the one time. His eyes adjusted to the light, and he embraced his son like two old souls, together, equal and kindred. They spoke without words for what felt like an eternity, although less than a minute had passed. I embraced my eldest son, and the pain of losing him, the tragedy, the drilling accident, the lifetime of mourning was now clear.

My mother, father and son walked with us back out onto the main Parish Road, my father wiping the sweat from his square, olive brow with his forearm and my mother waving a white cloth as the cortege left the townland of Keelogs, like standing out waving to a passing wedding procession with ribbons on the car instead of wreaths. Con put his hand on his son's shoulder and apologised for leaving them early, explaining that a lifetime could be one day or a hundred years, either way, it was a lifetime. He sent him back to TirConnell, back to his real life as far as the world was concerned, back to reality. They would meet again in the blink of an eye. The last of the men that had the rights to do so in the procession of carrying, stopped and ceremoniously placed me in the black hearse. I was being driven to my final resting place.

Chapter 7

"Have you seen the amount of muck on the roads this last while?" Tadhg walked between the two men. Their smokes blew bright orange in the wind. "The cut of the roads in Donegal, makes ye wonder if the Donegal County Council knows that roads have been cut in the Parish yet, we're that far behind the times". Pat Gavin threw the last of his tailor-made smoke butt over the hedge. It hissed black and damp immediately. Dan straightened his yellow coat and brushed ash from his lapels.

"Roads are getting worse Tadhg", he agreed. "God knows they are, ye take yer life into yer own hands just walking them, never mind the grazing on the long acre anymore."

"For sure," Tadhg replied and followed on. "You haven't seen or heard tell of anyone rallying the roads this past while, sure someone will get hurt — sooner or later", he appealed to their sense of right and wrong now.

"The young fellas have been fairly quiet since Eamonn Devenney went to London", Pat nodded forward at the hearse to indicate he was my grandson and swished the greasy hair from his eyes.

"Although he drove too fast, it was always great to get a lift to the town to save the old feet, madman as he was."

He sneered, almost jovial in the thought that it was Tadhg that informed the Guards about the lapsed insurance and the fine that sent the young fella to London to pay it off. Today wasn't a day to speak ill of me or my family, so Dan walked on ahead and was glad to be out of the company of the two lowlife blackguards. He felt immediately better after departing and vowed to keep away from them for the rest of the day. When he was fully out of earshot, Pat leaned down to Tadhg and whispered, "whist now and cm'ere te a tell ye, there was two cars going mad up the Planting yesterday evening, Derry and Dublin registered cars, if you're looking for a bit of information now, do you know what a mean and ye never heard it from me". He looked down at his feet and walked with a humble and contrite heart like a proper man of God, from the teeth out only.

"Very interesting Pat, very interesting indeed, and where did you come on this news or did you see them yourself?" he asked, excited now, unable to contain his happiness, he almost skipped and missed a step at the Cockhill bridge. Brown, brackish, nutrient rich water gargled furiously under the arches after leaving the hills of the Illies, not waiting to get to Buncrana and freedom again in the Swilly.

"I didn't see them, although I know one was a blue Cortina and not sure on the Northern yok. I overheard Dan Dotton tell it when we were sitting up this morning, nearly cleaned him off the road into the bargain a heard. His best yellow coat wrecked, slipped on the moss ye know what I mean. Cm'ere, mind you, ye never heard it from me, say no more, say no more, hold yer tongue, whist hold yer tongue", Pat replied and held out two nicotine stained fingers for another smoke as Tadhg reached for his twenty Carrolls. They stood with their backs to the wall of the old graveyard, savouring the intel, and sent plumes of sweet smoke into the clouds.

"One more thing Pat", Tadhg squinted like he had a glass eye, like he was Lieutenant Columbo, "off the record now, was the Northern car a green Vauxhall Cavalier by any chance?"

He butted out the smoke and they sauntered to the back of the Chapel. Pat stooped down to the level of the Altar Boy's ear and whispered, "cm'ere sur, whist hold yer tongue, a believe it was".

The Chapel was packed to overflowing. The only pews left were the wide seats that held the columns for the gallery above. They were dear bought, annoying to sit in and impossible to kneel on. Tadhg stood, daydreaming of another job well done at the end of the pole pew with his arms folded, smug as a lord in the sea of black suits. Surely, despite his small stature, he'd get a gig in the Garda Siochana if it meant two for the price of one. He was trying to prove that good intelligence gathering had nothing to do with being six feet tall, and the sooner that rule changed the better. He wanted to wear the uniform of his dreams with pure pride in front of his mother, with the deep voiced authority to go with it. Suddenly, he felt a weight on his left shoulder and a hoarse, gruff whisper, warm and steamy in his red ear.

"Push over there sur, plenty of room for ten men there."

He looked up at Paddy Poteen, smiling down through gritted teeth, like he was about to relieve Tadhg of a few of his own, chapel or not. Tomorrow was Saint Patrick's Day, a day that Lent could be broken, and sins didn't count and every man in Ireland could do his pleasure, whatever his heart desired, to drink poteen or to drown the shamrock, or simply kill or maim an informer. Tadhg's heart was racing, and the chapel suddenly became a hot sauna of warm muffled crowd and steamy breaths. His face was red as a beetroot and sweat ran down his spindly back. Paddy held the Altar Boy's head inside a pint of Guinness in his mind's eye as the priest started the Mass. He struggled to get out, frothing black and white and spluttering until the pint was dry, and he lay in there, looking out from behind the glass, a drunken monkey, a bother to no one, panting, squelched, distraught, and caught, begging for forgiveness. Paddy looked down at the wee man and smiled, quare head on him there, full of chaff.

For a minute, and only a minute, Tadhg thought about saying nothing. He knew that his information sharing with the Mayo mafia was well known and even documented in spray paint on the front wall of his house occasionally. The man sitting beside him with the death stare that would frighten the grim reaper, Paddy Poteen Ennis, knew of his secret life and felt the consequences. The men in blue had knocked his door with a search warrant for illegal liquor as Paddy stepped out into the frost. The house was rough to begin with. Every press, garment, loose floorboard, crevice, mouse hole, rat hole, the ceiling and outhouses, everything overturned, until finally, as Paddy knew they could have gone straight to, the side panel of the bath and the secret frame of the double bed, netting some three hundred bottles in total. They took photos of themselves pouring the bottles of spirits one by one into the brook with twenty that didn't make it, warming the hearts of elderly Mayo men after their Christmas dinner. The photo on the front page of the Derry Journal on the Friday before Christmas was a warning to any other budding entrepreneur in the district: the boys in blue could step on their throats at any time, they were always in charge, even if they looked the other way for the most part, they had ways and means of controlling their brethren in the North West. The Altar Boy was their main man.

A wee Derry woman from the Creggan sat at the tuppence slot machine in Mickey Carey's Amusements up the town street and fed it like a hungry child. Damn shame, she exclaimed, wiping the smoke from her eyes and spoke on the inward Rothmans drag to save time. Damn shame on the Guards, and a week before Christmas too, as she folded the Friday's Journal next to the machine, unable to look at the pure waste going on in the Republic and the pure destruction going on in Derry. She pulled on the lever with the black glossy knob with pure luck and hope. The bars and cherries lined up and Mickey Carey cried, only for a minute, and the tuppences rushed out into the tray, unable to hide their excitement, crashing against the silver base, turning everything bronze with free state coins. She waved across to her friend that had walked in from the cold as she waited on the tray to fill. "How's about ye?" she acknowledged her and cooeed for the attendant with the bucket to empty the stash of bronze bullion. Buncrana was the lucky country, except for the poteen man that day.

Chapter 8

My three sons and four daughters sat stoney faced in the front pew. Their husbands, wives and children filled the voids and gaps in the first four rows after that. Some from Derry, others from Birmingham, Chicago, Carndonagh and down the country, all well dressed and respectable, quiet and contrite: a united front of Devenneys, O'Duibhne in Gaelic, meaning black or descendant of the small black one. Speaking of black, I looked out on the crowd. John and Liam sat about ten rows back. It was enough for people to know they were part of the clan but far enough away that if Liam kicked off, which he would, then there may be some doubt as to who exactly they belonged to, black, white or indifferent. Liam was handicapped with cerebral palsy, spina bifida, epilepsy and the mental capacity of a four-year-old. There would be bother as strangers looked at the boy without a titter of wit. Paddy Poteen watched them from the pillar seat and knew exactly who they were, although he had only spoken to John a few times on the potato fields, he could see the stress on him as the shuffling stopped.

The priest spoke and there was deathly quiet, Big George quiet. The first time I ever got what I wanted, only now I didn't want it. It was too late to be careful of what I wished for. The peace and quiet turned to a literal deathly silence.

Liam started to fidget and pick his nose, looking at what came out, examining it and then rubbing it on John's trousers.

"Quit that sur", John whispered as the crowd rose as one and Liam remained sitting. "Get up sur, come on and there'll be the choc ice after like we said."

Liam planted himself in the pew, arms folded and defiant; thran, Devenney and Doherty thran, and awkward. He swished his arms and rubbed his nose on the cuff of his jacket. He finally stood beside his brother. "Will there be TV this evening, will there be? and will there be the news on, ye know the news, will there?"

He tugged at John's arm and, for the first time, finally noticed his closed left eye and the country stitching above it. "What happened yer eye John, what happened it, it's all cut and black sur?" he said, loudly enough for Paddy Poteen and the rest of the chapel to hear, as he reached to feel it. He had to see, touch and feel anything that was out of the ordinary. "My eye is grand Liam", John said as he pulled away with the pain, "I was stung by a wasp yesterday, but he's away now, flew off and died somewhere so no need to worry," he whispered to the best of his ability to keep him on side. The priest looked down on the crowd over his glasses as two of my grandchildren made their way up to the side pulpit for the first reading and the Responsorial Psalm.

Nothing charged the big cleric's batteries more than insolent chit chat during a Mass and especially two young fellas with not a manner between them. As if ye couldn't shut your gob for one hour a week, he thought, and more to the point, at a fucken funeral at that. I heard him. He noted where they sat and the cut of them. Bastards to hell as they were. Liam kept up the racket about the news and the rage built in the big man. He rocked backwards and forwards in his fine, soft black shoes and the lush carpet pressed heavy and groaned under his well-fed frame. He stared silently, hands up to his lips in meditative contemplation in their direction. The congregation waited silently in Big George, not a murmur, quiet as a church mouse style. I died a second time.

"There will be the news on this evening at half past five before I fodder the cows, but if there's any more carry on, there'll be no news. Now sit down there sur and don't move", John spoke quietly to the side of his head and the boy listened.

Liam was only three years younger but would always be a boy. He would never grow up. He would always, in this lifetime, belong to Tir Na Nog and the land of eternal youth. His body might age, whiskers grow thick and black and eventually grey on his face, and he may even duck his head to enter doorways, and belong to TirConnell like everyone else, but his mind and soul never would. It was, as I discovered in the past three days, the way it was meant to be, purely, simply, perfectly aligned, time and place, meant to be. He sat down, happy as the owner of Flaherty's pub on Saint Patrick's Day morning, pints on, lined up black and white with the brown drawer full of Irish punts and Derry Sterling. Tomorrow.

Communion time came. Kneeling, standing and everything in between, Liam had had enough. As they offered each other the sign of peace, the woman behind them smelling of strong perfume and with a bright, happy face, jet black hair and white, fresh teeth, tapped Liam on the shoulder to shake hands. He pulled away and refused.

"No way" and shrugged "not shakin hands th'day, that's all I'm sayin."

"Peace be with you", John held out his right hand, meekly, red faced, almost embarrassed.

Iris O'Malley smiled and saw through his brave front. "You'll be grand young fella, just grand, don't worry", she spoke softly and humanely, the words that I had been thinking.

It triggered him, cleared his mind of thoughts and things to do. He stood solidly on the ground; oak tree roots burrowed to the centre of the earth, and the eggshells that he was afraid to crumble on a daily basis, disappeared from under his feet. The events of the past wheen of days that would change his life were unbelievably real. The Druid Queen, in all her splendour and mystical glory, her beauty, the fairies that gathered to save his life and the events in the forge. He sat with it all and wished me well on my journey from TirConnell, as Liam pulled the inside of his trouser pocket out, dropping three white stones from my street onto the pew.

The crowd ambled slowly to communion and John nudged Liam with his knee to get up. Two of the stones dropped on the kneeboard and clattered loudly as the boy wiped his nose on his sleeve again. A white line appeared on the cuff of his coat like a slugs trail on bitumen. Liam was old enough. He had made his first communion and was bound to receive like everyone else, committing a mortal sin was as serious for him as the next man, whether he knew it or not, or cared, was another matter. Liam's limp was only slight. When you knew, you knew, and it was easy to spot. His right heel was raised, only allowing his toes to touch the floor. It moved him from side to side, like the swaying of a man leaving Flaherty's.

They made it to Father Doherty and John prodded Liam forward to the big man in white and to open his mouth. The priest grimaced, placing the communion firmly on the boy's tongue, as if pressing manners on him, a bit of shush, in the name of Christ, in Christ's house, for Christ's sake, pull your fucken head in. I stood beside them and couldn't help but laugh. Jesus had a chuckle as well since it was all part of his plan. Everything was perfect. John got similar treatment. His left eye was now almost fully closed and the plimsolls, wet from the shower of rain earlier, left black polish residue on the soft carpet. He took off quickly after his brother or he'd end up in the wrong seat. The chief mourners in the front pew shook their heads at the cut of them. Their mother, my daughter-in-law, Betty, was embarrassed in the second row. She had been to more funerals in the past three years than Mrs Kennedy in Massachusetts. She asked herself what in under God was John doing yesterday, not that she had hardly seen any of them since my wake started.

Paddy Poteen followed the boys back to their seat and sat next to John.

"It's John, isn't it?" Paddy asked, as Liam started jiggling the white stones in his pocket again. "Aye, that's right Paddy", he replied and pushed his feet under the kneeling board. He was happy that a man like Paddy knew his name.

"I knew your father well, John. We were in Scotland and Wales together, I can tell you a few things when you're older if you'd like, ye know sur, I could watch yer back."

Paddy looked into my grandson's eyes and his mad stare softened. A smile broke across his face, and he realised it might have been his first one of the year.

"Do ye need help now sur, whatever happened ye?" he asked and looked at the mess above his eye, black, swollen and sore.

"If I told you, you wouldn't believe it", John replied.

"You'd be amazed at what I'd believe, times that are in it. Don't tell me here, not now, come out to my house in the Backhill tonight and whatever needs fixing will be fixed, do ye know what I mean sur?"

Paddy felt relief that apart from the split over his eye, the young Devenney looked no worse for wear. He felt the spirit of John's father sitting between them with his arms around his two sons. Apart from that morning in the forge, he would keep his distance and wouldn't interfere again.

The Mass was over, and the crowd made their way out silently, with only a wheen of whispers here and there. Paddy walked away from the boys and made his way down the side aisle. The Altar Boy thought he saw them together but couldn't be sure. He stood on his tip toes to look towards the front. Damn pillars and five-foot nothing stance. He knew Paddy kept his business to himself. If he had been speaking to young Devenney, whatever his name was, there was a reason and he'd make it his business to find out.

Liam crunched through the hard chocolate coating of the choc ice outside Cullen's shop. Of all the things he couldn't do for himself, he was expert at cleaning a choc ice, neatly and with purpose, down to the stick without dropping a morsel. He handed John the stick as they walked over the Cockhill bridge towards Keelogs again. John smiled and went to the Illies side and leaned over the stone wall. "Go to the other side Liam and see if you can see it", he dropped the white stick into the fast flow. "I see it, I see it, a boat John, heading for the town", they both laughed and ran the two miles home.

Tadhg got into his dark blue Chrysler Avenger. It was ex-Gardai from Dublin. The screw holes for the two-way were roughly patched before the Dublin auction. The car smelt and felt Gardai, and locals gave him a wide berth. The taxi man in the town street had two of these cars. He carted drunk men home and middle-aged, scarf-wearing women with their shopping wherever they needed to go, normally to the countryside, to the Parish and the Illies. It squeaked with a full load of paying customers at a pound a go. He got the Donegal wave and smile despite the registration. Tadhg's car could be seen coming from half a mile away on a dark night, although it wasn't always easy to see the driver behind the wheel. He made a phone call outside the General's shop and dialled Tom O'Malley.

"Meet you at the usual place in ten minutes", he spoke directly and matter of fact on official Garda business.

-

"What have ye for me, what?" Tom asked Tadhg, as they walked along the shore front next to McCarterś factory. "There was a second car Tom, a blue Mark III Cortina with Dublin plates, and a fair chase up through the Parish."

"Very interesting Tadhg.. We have it from our brothers at Brigend that Dinny Hegarty left Derry three days ago and hasn't been seen since. There's a couple of places he could be, but my guess is that if the boys haven't killed him, then he's still in the Parish. How many places could he be? What? Whatever plans you had for the next week, cancel them, find me Dinny and you'll be on the payroll. Five foot nine to join, my arse, what, you're the best detective in Donegal."

Tom looked down at Tadhg but not down to him. He had grown to like the man, the chances he took and the predicament he was in. This job wasn't for everyone, and he was glad to have someone on his side. He turned the oversized lapel of his leather jacket against the next heavy March shower from Rathmullan. They ran for the cars and took off in opposite directions. Two factory workers ran to get back to McCarter's before the downpour and made it inside from their lunch break as the heavens opened. Hard, heavy, cold hail battered the asbestos roof. They looked out as both men pulled away. Margaret and Mary Mulligan looked at each other. Yer man was up to something, and their brother Peter, The Holy Father, would be told before the night was out.

Chapter 9

"Turn the aerial towards Rathmullan Liam, that's right, a bit that way, hold on, no, Jayses sur, one job sur, one job. The other way. That's it, hold it there and we can pick up RTE and UTV at the same time."

John gave the directions every evening until the frequency was just right, until he was in the zone, ready for the nightly news. Liam laughed and took his seat in the car shed. The wind from the Lough caught the loose aluminium arms of the aerial and it shook like a wonky hatstand at Casey's Drapers on the town street. The nightly news was the best part of the day; Liam lived for it and could be coaxed to behave almost anywhere at the mere mention of it.

John sat behind the frame of a brown PYE television. It came to Keelogs just before their father died and it somehow carried the remnants of his soul. Betty called it a relic of old decency. The TV, like the toasters, electric kettles, fridges, irons or anything else that came to the house, was either second-hand and still going but only just, second-hand and not going but could maybe be fixed if you were in any way handy, or a mixture of both. The TV came from Jack Porter's when they got a new one. It was the best day Keelogs had ever seen, as ornaments and memoriam cards were moved off the sideboard to make way for this wonderous piece of engineering. It went for about three hours until it got too hot and thick black lines rose from the sideboard, distorting the characters on the screen and disappearing into the sky above the timber frame. As the days went on, the watching time got less and less and the lines got faster, almost hypnotically so, to the point that when you looked away, the room was spinning and the China dogs on the mantlepiece started barking. Con took the back off on one of his rare trips home.

"Fucken tube ye see boys, ye know what a mean, it's the tube, always the tube with these yoks, a wouldn't buy them if they were on sale", he titched with his tongue against the roof of his mouth and shook his head at how nothing ever lasts, although Flaherty's pub had the best TV in the town, colour picture, cool tube, no lines and a remote to change the stations without getting up off the chair.

Betty said that Con owned it personally and should take it home with him to Keelogs. It fell on deaf ears.

"Give me a hand here boys", Con said, and it got thrown up the garden with everything else. It was to be one of the last times they saw him. After his funeral, John set the TV up in the car shed, next to the turf for the fire. He carefully took the back off, the tube out and the screen off, leaving the timber frame and knobs and nothing in between but fresh air and the unique smell of dry Donegal turf.

"Two, one, action!"

Liam sat far enough away to see his brother, the newsreader, and he stomped his feet on the gravel of the street in anticipation. John started.

"Good evening and welcome to the five o'clock Keelogs news on RTE 1. It's Monday the 16th of March, 1981. Charles Mitchell can't be here this evening, he's setting perdies in a field outside Dublin and I'm standing in. Here are the headlines as I see them. Big George Devenney got buried in Cockhill today. There was such n' a big crowd that the gallery was heaving as well and standing room only at the back and outside. People came from far and wide and even the vet showed up. Aye, George Devenney was hard as nails, and thran beyond words, but he was well loved and he was our Granda. Dan Dotton said it was the biggest funeral hed ever seen and with the good heavy shower when he was at the foot of the lane, the angels were crying too at the loss of him."

John straightened himself and lightly patted his left eye with the palm of his hand. He peered out at his brother taking it all in, silently, enjoying, listening — the nightly routine.

"In other RTE news, it has been reported that Willie John McLaughlin has dug the biggest hole with a JCB digger that Donegal has ever seen. Willie John is the finest operator in the country for cesspools, foundations or big stones in the field. Some locals have complained about the size of the hole and called the Garda Siochana to come out and investigate, they're looking into it, the hole that is."

"What, John what do you mean?" Liam smiled and asked again to no reply.

John stood above the TV. "I canny see you Liam, do ye mind that, mind I told ye. You can look in and see me, but when I'm looking out, I can neither see nor hear you, it's the frequency." Liam looked puzzled and gestured for his brother to keep going regardless.

I sat on a chair next to Liam and was happy to still be there. I laughed with my grandsons and was the first to admit my stubbornness, holding onto a pound note like it was the last one I'd ever see. And just like the TV, with John looking out, I could see in but they could neither see nor hear me, but they knew I was there and carried on as if I were part of the audience. At the foot of the lane by the two large white pillars, directly in line with the big rock on Stragill shoreline, the Queen stood and looked up at the nightly news. Forever connected in the land of TirConnell, the greatest story being told was their own and she honoured it. The news carried on...

"And now for sport and weather. Bob Paisley, the Liverpool manager has given the team a wheen of days off from a tight playing schedule and they're foundered in the wild weather. If you look across the Lough to Rathmullan, you can see all the weather coming from their direction, but in short, not good weather for cutting turf. Take an umbrella, if you have one."

Liam walked over and moved the dial on the top right-hand corner of the box. He walked back to his chair and took up his position again. UTV news.

John started the news and mouthed the words without sound.

"I canny hear ye, John, I canny hear a word." Liam sat sideways on the broken blue chair with no back.

John stood up and spoke to his brother over the brown box. "Did you turn down the volume on that knob sur?"

"Aye, maybe I did", Liam replied.

"Well, turn it back up if you want to hear anything from Ulster", he laughed and sat back in position. "Good evening Ulster and welcome from Keelogs. Making news this evening, Bobby Sands is mid-way through his third week on a hunger strike in the Maze, after starting on 1st March. We at Keelogs stand with him and wish him well. Hopefully it will all be called off soon."

Liam had no idea what was just said and sat quietly fidgeting, waiting for the funny part, but the Queen edged closer and sat under the ash tree, partly like she'd heard it for the first time and partly because she was the reason that John was now able to speak beyond his years, beyond his lot in life, beyond expectations and beyond his Cockhill school education. She watched the live TV for the first time. As she looked to the heavens, he saw her there and she spoke telepathically of how she'd seen every invader for the past five thousand years, come and go and live and die, believing they owned something, something physical when they died helpless, penniless, and alone, like me with two pockets full of Atlantic air. Rain fell heavily on the gravel around her, but she remained dry and untouched.

The wind swirled up from the Lough and Rathmullan disappeared into a grey mist on the far side. The tentacles of the cloud dropped black and grey and sideways on the water as the frontal breeze shook the budding branches of the ash tree above the audiences' heads. The boys didn't notice any change in the weather and felt no cold or spots of rain. Dry turf mould at the entrance to the open car shed swirled and rose up from the ground, flying into the crevices of the loose stone walls. It smelt like moss and heather; it smelt like home and always would, like a coal fire to a Welsh man. A feeling of warmth came over the boys, like laying in the lower bedroom on a stormy night as the wind heaved in from the Atlantic, and rain pelleted against the glass like machine gun fire — curtains blowing and the great turf fire on. Flames danced on the timber ceiling and reams of peeled wallpaper on damp walls cast ghostly shadows in the corners. With heavy blankets and old army coats for extra weight, it was a safe place with the four brothers and the old lodger from Drumfad, it was a time to tell stories, stories of the potato fields, stories of TirConnell, Donegal.

The newsreader wiped away the dust and finally Liam moved position to be out of the squall without taking his eyes off his brother. The news continued...

"News just in", John grabbed a piece of paper from between the stones. "News just in from Derry City Council, there was a load of false faces that went missing at Halloween last year and haven't been seen since. The Altar Boy has informed them that Liam Devenney has been wearing one since then and hasn't taken it off. If anybody should see Liam, can ye get him to take off the false face for people in the Parish are getting the wild scare and cows are not milking because of it." John put the paper back in the crevice and smiled, waiting on the wrestle.

"I am not wearing no false face, John", Liam made a beeline for the TV and all three hit the ground together. "Ye can see me now, I bet ye, oh ye can see me now John, yer not in the TV now sur and no false face." The brothers laughed and roared as the Queen disappeared quietly down the lane, making ready for the celebration of the Spring Equinox.

"Yer head's marley Liam", John laughed.

"Your head's marley, John, ye have a quare big head on ye there, full a chaff."

The brothers wrestled in the turf dust. "Quit yer gurnin' and neamin'", John laughed playfully with his brother.

The dog joined in the melee. He was a large mongrel called Andy and arrived smelling of cow dung and fox holes after being thrown out of a car at the bottom of the Parish. He was rejected at each farmhouse until he got to Keelogs. His loyalty to the Devenneys was absolute and his life was given over to protecting Liam. He threw the ball for him against the low walls of the street every day. When the ball was lost, which was most days, Liam threw stones for him to catch. His front teeth were broken as he caught the stones and he pulled at John's shirt with bare, baldy gums, exactly like my own.

Betty looked out the front window at her two youngest sons and smiled. It was the first time she had caught herself smiling in six months and her blue eyes sparkled directly from the dusting of love in her heart, lighting up her beautiful, youthful-looking, peachy face. She had a warm, radiant glow, an earthly warm TirConnell glow that came from giving life to seven children on this land, connected, grounded, each one welcomed like the last, loved, cared for and now all but two gone.

The flame in her heart had all but extinguished, the candle melted, vanished, and the pungent smell of the white smoke brought her into another world. My world. The lights stayed off inside until the last ray of sun had passed, like any Donegal country house. The dark echoes of the past cast her slender body in a hazy shadow on the kitchen floor from the dying light of the day. In the still silence, she prayed to God for guidance. She looked up at the dusty Sacred Heart of Jesus portrait with the red eternal flame light under it, looking down on her with sorrowful, mournful eyes, yet full of compassion for her predicament, two open palms, nail hole marked for his trouble, giving her strength. She stood like a ghost in the farmhouse kitchen, a dark shadow behind the white curtains in what was her father's house. The only house she had ever known, although there were others that she either couldn't remember, or had blocked out of her mind for good reason. I stood there with her, watching my grandsons and, on the other side of her stood Jesus himself, with a love more powerful than any words could describe. We watched the Queen leave beyond the white pillars; she acknowledged us and sent us love.

Betty worried too much, much more than was ever needed. The things she worried about kept coming true like a prediction of doom, like a physic telling her own future, writing her own life's story and what could go wrong, should go wrong and would go wrong. She blamed herself for Con's death, the reason he was in the tunnels, sending money home from London, Liverpool, Aberystwyth, Scotland, and any other Godforsaken hole in the ground that tunnel men, drillers and blasters spend their time. If only, she thought. If only. She imagined him standing there and holding her. Strong, dark, handsome, his forehead glistening in the light and pure mad though, mad as a cut snake, mad as a Donegal Tiger, but her Donegal Tiger, her only partner and husband.

"Murder, look at the cut of these boys, get rid of all yer jump the bullocks now, ye pair of bastards".

Old Jack O'Donnell, the lodger, stood on the step, holding his night-time po and watched the melee in the car shed. He was aged somewhere between seventy-nine and one hundred. Even now, speaking from this side, I have no idea how old he is, God and Jack still kept some secrets from me. He still stood over six feet tall, somewhat bandy-legged and with a slow gait. He wore a green checked suit from Casey's Drapers and a Donegal tweed cap covered a full head of white hair, apart from a pope's cap on his crown. His left eye drooped red and gawdy and he told young Liam that he got the injury sparring with Cassius Clay. He had a long nose, straight and sharp and his wrinkles were soft and white, almost non-existent until he frowned, when furrows like potato field drills formed across his forehead. He could have thatched the house with women in his heyday but for two old aunts in Drumfad that thwarted his efforts to bring a girlfriend home. These aunts lived excruciatingly long lives, so long in fact that by the time they departed to my side of the fence with their sunken eyes glowering out of the outshot bed, Jack himself was an old man and the women required to thatch the house were wives of other men. He made do when he realised he'd be a bachelor for life, although it tainted his outlook and when the only spinsters left were devout seamstresses from the factory with no need of men only to milk the cow or cut and dry turf, or women that looked like they'd been pulled through a hedge backwards with binder twine, his days of thatching the house with women were over.

He was cantankerous and, yes, like myself, thran as a donkey on derby day, but he was a Godsend to that house, and I never thought I'd hear myself say it. We were, shall we say, less than friendly to each other when I was there, and a chance meeting at a crowded wake or at the cattle mart was a familiar nod or a lukewarm wave at best. We spoke from the teeth out, or in my case, from the baldy gums out.

Chapter 10

Dinny Hegarty waited all day in the poteen den. He had smoked twenty Carrolls before lunchtime and kept a close eye on his watch. The funeral would be over by now surely. Where the hell was Paddy with news? He pictured a local man in his mind's eye, cranky as a bag of cats that his best milking cow lay mortally injured, blood spilling onto the road with a hole in her side the size of a football, being put out of her misery with the shotgun on the side of the Planten Road and the culprit, well, the culprit with a bounty on his head, never to be forgiven. The other scenario played a lot worse for Paddy and couldn't be fixed. If it was a person that he'd hit∴his heart sank deeper than the wreck of the Laurentic and with the same dire consequences. He imagined the name being given out at the funeral today, their family bawling in anguish, gritted teeth, sad and angry, baying for revenge or someone prayed for, being *a waiting* on, battered, bruised and dying. He shouted at the voices to stop, but they only multiplied and shouted louder.

His heart raced like he was going out on a volunteer mission, but at least on a mission he had some control. Today, he was helpless. He must sit, hide and wait. He emptied drums of water reserved for poteen and boiled a black kettle on the gas. He drank tea and smoked more until his windpipe felt black and glazed, like the inside of a stone chimney in a thatched house. In the cold light of Saint Patrick's Day eve, he took the tarp off the Cortina and examined the damage, throwing himself on the bonnet to emulate the dents that were there. It was definitely less than a cow and maybe more than a person. He would never drink again. Spots of red, maybe blood, sprinkled lightly on the roof and the boot, although it was hard to make out with the dried muck, hardened over the blue paint and windswept scratches of every branch and briar in the Parish. If only, he protested, if only he could fully remember. 'If only' were the loneliest two words in the English language and in this thought he connected with Betty in Keelogs making the same lament.

She somehow felt his prompt from Augaweel and the thought of the cut above John's eye left her wondering how it happened. He hadn't answered when asked earlier in the day and she felt shame, pure shame, at the cut of him and Liam at communion today. It was like no one owned them. Her heart sank. She owned them, and one day they would make her so proud that her heart would almost explode with love. The door opened and John left two fresh buckets of water from the Drumfad River spout on the bench in the scullery. He rushed back out again before she had the chance to speak.

"I'm away and will be back at half nine or so", he grabbed his coat from the front hall on the way out and blessed himself from the holy water font inside the front door. There was something telling him he may need it. He free-wheeled down Keelogs brae on his latest bicycle acquisition from the potato field barter system. There were reasonable front brakes on this one, while the back brake cable was non-existent and the jaws of the brake pad frame were opened wide, like someone with their mouth open getting a wild scare or a donkey about to neigh. It sat on the bicycle frame like an ornament in Betty's kitchen.

John could hear the sound of a car in the distance, being driven slowly and carefully. He glanced quickly over his shoulder and made out the blue Avenger belonging to the Altar Boy. For whatever reason, he knew to keep off his radar and pedalled hard, leaving the townland of Keelogs like an athlete and the slim tyres of the racer barely had a chance to touch the road as he slowed just enough to turn up Druminor Road. He pulled in tight behind a ditch and stopped, gassed and panting.

The Avenger drove purposely past the intersection with the driver looking up at an empty road, apart from a small black rabbit huddled out of the wind and twitching her ears. Tadhg thought he'd seen the boy but couldn't be sure. It felt good to be on official Garda business. He pulled the seat even further forward and put down the window. His would-be special branch leather jacket smelt of success and he put his elbow out the window, surveying all that he seen around him, all that belonged to him and him alone. He felt like the six-million-dollar man and decided to wait for the full cover of darkness before going to the Backhill. It was bandit country with one road in and out. It wasn't to be taken lightly, and they knew him well, well enough that if they came on him during the course of his surveillance, it wouldn't end well. He'd die the dastardly death of a thousand screams. He decided to leave the car in a quiet laneway and walk out, taking cover if he met a car.

John put his hand up to knock on the open door and called from the step.

"Come in John, a have ye now, a have ye, a know ye, safe enough surely, you don't knock on the door here, just walk on in sur, that's the Backhill way and you're as welcome as the flowers in May, always will be here, any son of Con, ye know sur. Sorry about your old fella too. Come in, come in."

Paddy ushered John into the kitchen like Petesie with a torch at the cinema on a Saturday night moving people to the right seat. He moved a cardboard box of messages from the sofa and, with an old Friday's Derry Journal, swished dirt from a hard chair next to it. He lifted the chair as if it was a feather, putting it down with authority close to the fireplace, away from the window and any prying eyes. The poteen man was making no sense to himself, John or me, he was just nervous energy and although he had been a boy of around the same age with Con in Scotland, with no work, starving and stealing turnips from fields to survive, being chased by policemen telling them get back to Ireland, he didn't have the same rapport with my grandson, not yet anyway and an IRA man's life depended on his building one, and quickly.

"Thanks for coming out here John, we can have a quiet chat away from the crowd. So, what happened your eye? Like you were saying, what? I wouldn't believe ye. Tell me sur." Paddy sat backwards on the hard chair by the fireplace and placed his chin on the backrest. His piercing eyes stared kindly at John and his long stubble rested on the tops of his hands. John felt the cut above his eye with the soft of his left palm. It throbbed in pain and felt hot to touch.

"Paddy, I got knocked down last night down near the Planting Bridge, I don't know what kind of car it was. I heard nothing and stupid enough was tying my lace in the middle of the road. Next thing, I was tumbling through the air. I felt dead, I'm sure I was dead."

Paddy poteen listened intently, and apart from the clock ticking slowly and methodically on the wall, there wasn't another sound. There was an awkward silence for what seemed like ten minutes but was only five seconds; neither wanted to say too much, to be the first to speak or make any sense of it.

Paddy rubbed his chin against the chair back and looked at John directly. "It's like this sur, I know the man that knocked ye down, and it's complicated."

Johns' eyes widened. He breathed in to speak. Words on the tip of his tongue stayed there and got no further. He should have felt anger but didn't.

Paddy lit a cigarette and continued. "He was being chased by Crown forces at the time and didn't realise what he'd hit or if he'd hit anyone at all. He's very sorry about it and whatever can be done to make this right, will be done, ye know what I mean now sur, whatever ye need."

John remained silent and took a minute to think on it. The clock ticked. There was an air of authority in this house, although a rough camp, messy, male, unkempt — it was a house that bowed to no man and was happy in its own skin, and a place where normal rules and laws did not apply. The light from the kitchen shone yellow rays on the swaying hawthorn branches outside.

"I accept the apology, Paddy." John looked directly into the red-hot turf fire. "I accept but I need something in return, I need a job, any kind of job to help in the house, do you know of anything?" He looked directly at Paddy now, a proposal more than a question.

"What do you know about poteen making?" Paddy asked.

"Nothing, but I know most of the men in the potato fields that drink it and they're half demented", he replied and laughed.

"Well, sur, that's good enough for me, ye can be trusted, ye'll never be suspected and you're a son of Con's. I have work for ye. Now, tell me, what did you say I wouldn't believe in the Chapel for I'm afraid of nothing on two feet and very little on four."

The poteen man laughed and scratched through his hair, the pressure lifted: the deal was done.

"All I can remember is being lifted out of the muck with many small hands and sat by the wall of the Planting Bridge. I was broken, my arms and legs felt like they weren't mine anymore and I couldn't move. Then she appeared."

"Who?"

"The Queen, the Druid Queen, surrounded by twelve fairies. They healed everything except this cut above my eye", John replied.

"That sounds unbelievable alright sur, but I know her too. Ye don't spend as much time as me out in the wilds and taking shortcuts through hazel and blackthorn Plantings not to have seen her myself. You're a lucky man to have met her this early in life. So lucky sur, she has ye marked for something or ye'd have been let go on, ye know what a mean, to the light, ready for the Banshee to cry."

Paddy felt vindicated for all his years of solitary madness, his unwavering belief in the fairies and the Druid Queen, and now, well now, the confirmation that it was true. He had living proof. Paddy looked youthful, playful, almost radiant when he smiled, and he decided to do it more often. My grandson, John Devenney, was to be the lifeline he needed, a reason to get up in the morning, a surrogate son, in need of a mentor, friend, accomplice. Serendipity was alive and well in the Backhill.

"Ye can start tomorrow, after the Mass at Cockhill. I have three gas bottles that needs to be refilled and there's things to do out at the still. I'll keep ye going, and ye'll get to meet Dinny, the driver, are ye right with that?" he asked, looking directly at John's left eye and wondered why she left it untreated and ugly.

"That's ok Paddy, no harm done, I'm sure we'll get on", John replied and was glad to get the job.

He remembered the last time he saw his father and although it was somewhat slurred after a day in Flaherty's, it went something like *take yer tricks when ye get them, and an honest day's work rarely yields an honest pay when some bastard has deep pockets in front of ye, life's unfair, take yer dealer's trick early in life and bow to no man.*

John left the Backhill house, and his eyes adjusted quickly to the darkness. He pedalled out the laneway, dodging potholes in the wheel ruts and the muddy grass in the centre. There was money being made in the poteen operation but, in true Paddy style, there was nothing palatial about his house. The rougher the laneway looked, the less likely anyone would suspect he was making money and that was just how he liked it. The birch trees stood on either side like goalpost markers. There was no need of a light; it attracted unwanted attention and you either knew where you were going, or you didn't. John was happy and I moved alongside him. I was happy too and tried to warn him what was waiting but couldn't interfere. A bicycle always feels like it's going faster on a dark night, almost like it's being propelled by someone else when you can't see your own legs. It was a luxury to have two pumped up tyres under you and John felt excited and nervous at the same time about the job, fully aware that, even though the money was needed, Betty would have a conniption if she found out that Paddy Ennis, Paddy Poteen, a non-believer, dissenter, Druid, heathen and jailbird was her benefactor.

The moon rose quickly above Lough Swilly and appeared from behind the Rathmullan Mountains where she had been hiding since the cloudy weather last Friday. Millions of incandescent lights sprinkled on the lough like opening night at the pantomime shining on the main character. Dark shadows were cast over the Backhill, but the road perpendicular to the lough, the only way out, had the same glow as the lough. John emerged from the darkness and turned left to freewheel down the hill. The spokes of the front wheel shone bright and silvery in the light. He looked down at their turning and pedalled faster, silently, then he eased off and the free wheel cog rattled like a fast-moving combination lock at the bank. He took his hands off the handlebars and I shouted out to deaf ears. A dark shadow jumped from the ditch like a black ghost and poked a stick into the front wheel. For the second time in three days, John went tumbling through the air as the back wheel rose above his head. He landed with his two hands breaking his fall onto the rough bitumen. The bike clanged and scraped along the ground, steel on stone, bending, stripping spokes, worse than wrecked. He felt sure there was a stone that he didn't see, something. Whatever it was, he felt that familiar pain again and he lay groaning on the road, checking for scratches and scrapes in the new moonlight.

Suddenly, he felt a cold, wet foot on his throat as he struggled to get up. A torch clicked on, and the blinding rays were directly shone in his eyes. It was the Altar Boy.

"What's your name boy, no time for shite here, you're in big trouble, what's your name and what are you doing up here at night?" The accent put on, authoritative, like a big man from down the country, like a Guard or customs man or Gauger, or worse, a Mayo man. He was none of those.

John tried to move but the weight of the foot on his neck was blocking his windpipe. He felt like he was dying again. Rage mounted in him. No one was taking his life, and no one had the right to hurt him anymore. He had to think quickly. At least there only appeared to be one voice, so he had a fifty-fifty chance of fight or flight. He reached across hard with his sharp knuckles and buried his left fist into the assailant's calf. Tadhg roared in pain and the weight lifted from John's throat, enough for him to swing his left leg and kick the back of his knee out. In two seconds, both were in fighting position in the middle of the road. John danced left and right, light on his toes in the Donegal moonlight. He recognised the low set of the Altar Boy and ran at the bastard with speed, shoulder dropped, and hit him with all his might in the stomach. They both rolled into the brook along the road and exchanged punches in the glistening water. A warm flow blinded John's left eye and he swung at the black shadow with pure Devenney brute force. His olive skin glistened bright and oily in the moonlight. I stood there with him and kicked at the Altar Boy with a futile result, my efforts slicing through him without making a sound. His beautiful leather jacket was scratched, wet and mucky, but it shielded his kidneys from a pummelling. John had two older brothers and Liam younger. To not be able to fight in Keelogs was akin to the runt of the litter getting no food or a calf suckling the hind tit, empty and dry of milk. The Altar Boy's punches landed on John like soft, wet sponges and with the force of a butterfly. John moved in closer with no chance of being hurt. He smelt the informer's cheap aftershave, his leather, his fear and could hear his heart beating, thumping, scared. John battered him around each eye and held him up with his left elbow, dropping it away quickly, he threw an uppercut under his chin and heard the Altar Boys teeth chattering. The interrogation was over, no Garda information tonight.

Tadhg wasn't expecting the push back or the aggression from the young Devenney. He was meant to strike fear in his heart, to bully him into talking, to bring John to the level of himself, but he thought it better to run, live and fight another day and maybe, just maybe, he hadn't been recognised. He took off running through the gap in a field, disappearing like a black ghost on Halloween night.

John's heart settled and he washed his face in the icy cold brook, stemming the flow of blood. After five minutes, he collected his bike, or what was left of it, and walked it home with the front wheel raised and the back wheel rubbing on the frame at the same spot in every revolution. He picked the torch up from the middle of the road and put it in his back pocket as a memento, a trophy. He'd give it back to him one day soon, when he least expected it, hopefully to the side of the head. We walked down the hill together and he spoke to me as if I was physically there and I answered. I was the proudest grandfather in Ireland, in the world, in the universe, and I thanked the Christ light for this opportunity. I was having the time of my afterlife. There was nowhere else I would rather have been.

Chapter 11

John tapped on Cormac's bedroom window; he needed the Surgeon General again. Cormac opened the curtains and helped his mate in the small side window.

"What happened you? Again? Jese, John there's bark off you from asshole to breakfast time", he shook his head in disbelief. John's blood was dripping on the windowsill, he looked like, and essentially was, a casualty of war.

"It's a long story Cormac, have you any more of that black thread? I think your handiwork has been undone again. Sorry sur."

"You, sorry? If it wasn't for me, this would have never happened in the first place."

"I'm glad it did, sur, I'm glad it did."

John sat on the side of the bed for the second stitching, and they were clean out of fish fingers for freezing. He closed his eyes and thought of a united thirty-two counties, a united Ireland and a world without the Altar Boy, as the needle pierced him again and again, sharp and throbbing, prickly and painful.

John got back to Keelogs at eleven thirty and the light was off in the kitchen. He was glad he wouldn't have to see his mother, annoy her, worry her for no reason. He made his way to the lower room after having a piddle on the dewy grass and emptied the tank, save filling Jack's po in the middle of the night, and the roaring in the morning for the inquest as to who filled Charlie? He turned the doorknob slowly and the dim night light was barely enough to navigate past the mouse hole in the floorboards. The fireplace was dark, cold and empty, like a Derry woman's handbag leaving Mickey Carey's one-arm bandits. The room felt damp. It longed for the warmer days and a bit of druth as the wallpaper drooped lower each day, falling off the wet walls like a giant wave of outdated patterns and musty flowers. Old Jack swished the Rosary in his bed in the corner, his long Johns keeping his white, bandy frame warm. Deep in devoutness going through the decades, he could speak when the Rosary was finished, with his penance over. Conversation now would put him off and somehow lessen its potency.

Liam was comfortable under the mass of blankets and the big green army coat, laying in the well-worn dip in the middle of the bed, between the springs and frame. There was a perfect spot there and the young fella, slow and all as he was, could find it without trying.

"You're wild late home John", Liam spoke, almost sleep talking, and probably was.

"Shift over there sur", John whispered, as he gently pushed his brother across the bed. He lay his head down gingerly. Everywhere there was pain, there was heat and throbbing, everywhere except for the Altar Boy's punches. Pain, both physical and mental pain, had no hold over him. He laughed at it, made fun of it, giving it no power, there was always someone worse off. I taught him that since he was four years old, putting a halfpenny in the jam jar on a Friday at school for the black babies. If you had food in your belly, you could shite in the morning and a bed to lay your head at night, you were better off than most. He fell asleep with that thought and I discovered then that the rules of my engagement were not exactly black and white. I sat on the cold hearth and watched the occupants of the lower room fall asleep. I watched my grandsons' spirits rise and leave the room, free from time and gravity and I spoke to them openly and in great detail. Tomorrow morning, Saint Patrick's Day, our conversation would fade away into a forgotten dream, but the intention and the nudge would stay. I was more than happy with that.

-

Peter Mulligan rose early from the scratcher. His droopy, tired eyes cursed him for the rest of the day as they struggled to stay focussed. By eight o'clock, the white Sistine smoke rose from the Holy Father's fireplace. Parish men with three weeks of druth after being dry as a cornflake since Ash Wednesday, had one day and one day only to break Lent, and with three weeks' worth of drinking money under the bed, it had the hallmarks of a wild day. Thran men, mad women, angry men, quiet men, street angels and fireside devils would be at the door soon, which was which remained to be seen. Brigid Mary wiped the black counter of the bar and put change in the till. She glanced over at Peter and nodded silently towards the phone. "Call the boys", she said quietly, almost whispering, elbows on the bar. She detested trouble of any kind, and the unfriendly visit from the Guards the other night had unsettled her. She heard him dialling the Northern number and the unmistakeable sound of the dial springing backwards gave her goosebumps.

"It's Peter. We have a problem brewing out here", Peter spoke, and the other end remained silent, listening, calm, thinking.

"What's goin' on there, Peter? Our man didn't get to his destination after we spoke and hasn't been seen since, car's missing too", he replied.

"I am hearing reports he was seen and chased but no idea if he got away. The Guards were here last night, two special branch, they know nothing but they're fishin' and they know something's going on. The Altar Boy was seen speaking with Tom O'Malley yesterday down the shore front. They're watching, waiting. If Dinny is still alive, they're waiting on him to surface", the line went quiet for a while and the calm Dublin accent spoke directly, like a general directing troops.

"Go out to the Backhill, see if anything is stirring out there, and keep me informed."

The line went quiet again and he came back after thirty seconds. "Create a diversion, a couple of phantom calls, keep them busy today, although they'll be around the town for the parade, keep them busy in between and set that sting up, it's time, it's time to reel him in, he's not a good trout.

-

Tadhg jumped into the back seat and slammed the door. He wasn't a happy bunny and, for the first time ever, was less than amicable with his special branch brothers. They drove around the back road in Buncrana and headed down to the shore front. Apart from a few early Mass goers on this holy day of obligation, the roads were empty as people enjoyed the day off work. Ass's Teeth had been enjoying it too until the phone call from Tom at the sparrow fart early hour of eight o'clock. They parked up outside McCarters factory.

"What the hell happened you?" Tom looked at the cut of Tadhg, as if he'd just noticed his two black eyes and swollen nose and Mick echoed with "good God", as he feigned a yawn and exposed his donkey's ass teeth.

"I was keeping an eye on Paddy Ennis last night and they're up to something out there. That young Devenney was out there with him for over an hour."

Tadhg put down the window slightly and winced as the movement annoyed his ribs. His teeth were sore, all of them, a dull ache top and bottom.

"Keep going Tadhg, I mean, what happened you if you were only watching and reporting like we said? How did you end up like this, what?" Tom asked.

The Altar Boy's ego had taken a terrible battering. He felt like his short career was over before it had even begun, and he couldn't bear to tell the truth about last night and that young fella not yet fifteen. John would have to pay, he should have squealed like a pig and given the information when he was asked nicely. He opened the hateful gate, and allowed one fox and one Alsatian, mean, sharp and dripping blood, into the henhouse. His conscience was clear and, yes, this was a dirty business and he had friends in high places with low morals.

"I was watching the place like you said and saw the Devenney boy leave around ten o'clock. I decided to watch for another while when the young fella came up behind me and hit me with a timber paling post. I was out to it from the start and he kept punching and kicking me when I was on the ground. When I woke up, he was gone, that's the truth of it now."

Tadhg spoke with conviction, a man wronged, a victim from a heathen family, and all for the love of the Guards and Ireland.

Mick punched his fist into the palm of his other hand. "We'll see what Mr Devenney has to say for himself when he's lifted. I wonder if he's ever been punched through a phone book before. He's about to find out, see how smart he is then."

"There will be manners in Donegal before we leave it, what, that's for fucken' sure, what." Tom felt guilty for being tucked up in bed last night when this was going on and he assured Tadhg again that this would be dealt with, strongly and swiftly.

Chapter 12

"Who goes there, friend or foe?" Paddy Poteen called from the lower room, addressing the firm knock on the back door. The curtains were black in colour and black in every other way; not one shred of light penetrated the darkness. He had been in bed less than three hours after being out at the den with supplies of tea, bread, ham and smokes for his guest. He was careful not to be followed. If it was the Guards with a search warrant, they were duty bound to identify themselves. He waited for the Mayo accent, loud, authoritative, important, condescending, unapologetic, but they always came to the front door. Nothing happened, so he edged the curtain slightly and it was the man he was expecting.

"Right sur, a have ye, a have ye now, give me a minute", Paddy shouted, as he stumbled into his clothes and opened the door.

"You're a sight for sore eyes Peter, come in sur, come in." He rubbed sleep from his eyes and looked east and west, beyond the trees and bushes.

"I'll get straight to the point Paddy, have you seen Dinny Hegarty since Sunday?" Peter spoke in a low tone.

"I have him, and he's safe enough Peter, I have him in Augaweel since Sunday night. Couldn't come to see you until I worked out what had happened exactly, ye know what a mean sur, ye know what a mean."

Paddy was relieved to share this one-on-one. With phones tapped, cars being followed and informers watching, lives were at stake, and as the hunger strike dragged on in the Maze, it was a dangerous time all around. Paddy explained all about the chase and John on Sunday. They drank tea and worked out the way forward. Peter took four bottles of poteen from the trap door under the holly tree. All going well, Dinny would be moved by tomorrow, Mark III Cortina and all.

The Saint Patrick's Day Mass started at nine thirty sharp in Cockhill, but Peter Mulligan had lost faith in faith a long time earlier. He stood at the bottom of the Chapel Lane and took a moment to enjoy the smell of springtime, stepping from one foot to another, exercising, stretching, fidgeting, footering, waiting for his man to arrive. He watched the last stragglers make their way up the lane and knew that Ted was always late. Ted Hagen parked the car and reversed against the timber paling fence, along the bank of the Crana River. He quickly did the check, handbrake, in gear, smokes, matches and money. His wife, Angela, and weans piled out, more weans than there were seats for and definitely more than there were seatbelts for. Ted had no Catholic inclination or deep faith, except to go forth and multiply, and this he did better than any man I knew. At thirteen weans and counting, he had the policy of *one in her, one out of her and one ready to go in her* and he seriously enjoyed that part of Catholicism.

With Angela and the last of the weans safely disappeared inside the front door, Ted stood at the foot of the lane with Peter and lit up.

"Good to see you Peter, how have you been?" Ted smiled at his mate. They were close, like brothers. They grew up together, same class, same fights and pulled each other out of countless holes.

"Have you been on the job again sur? Jese no more weans, they'll have to build another school just for your tribe", Peter laughed.

"I need you to give me a hand today, Ted, no questions asked, and it won't be forgotten."

"Don't mention it Peter, whatever it is, it'll be done."

"Go and see yer wee mate, fill the boot with water and sprinkle a wheen of bottles of poteen in there amongst them, you know what I mean, don't you. I will drop the bottles behind your pillars on the way home. Has to be done today, they'll raid you and we'll be watching, I have to move a man while that's happening."

"Angela will go stone, stark, raving mad."

Ted pictured her screaming at the guards as they searched in the hot press, in the turf shed, under the weans' beds and the attic. Ted butted out his smoke and quietly slinked into the Chapel.

The priest was in the best form and happy to be celebrating the national saint. It was Father Bradley, a Donegal man himself from down about Killybegs. He made the people feel like being there, like they were getting some good out of the hour and they would leave the better for the experience. He started the sermon, and apart from a few light coughs and the heavy, chesty, familiar sound of old Jack near the back, he had their full attention.

I am reminded on this feast day and celebration of Saint Patrick that he was a great communicator with God in Heaven. He converted the High Kings of Ireland to the way of Christianity, stamping out paganism and false God rituals, therefore saving the souls of all who inhabit this land. He spoke regularly to Jesus when he was a slave here. It wasn't all one-way traffic though. It wasn't 'dial a Jesus' only when things were going bad but sharing the good times too, the happy times, celebrating his love of God. It brings up a story told to me by an Australian priest, Father Cressey, that stayed with me one time. He was from the old whaling port of Eden, on the far south coast of New South Wales, and he told me this story that still brings a smile to me:

Brigid was looking for a car park at the supermarket, but every spot was taken. No one seemed to be leaving and, try as she might, when she was the furthest distance away from one that did come up, another car would take it. Finally, as a Christian woman, she asked for the help of Jesus and Mother Mary in her quest. She kept driving around, frustrated, looking, red faced and getting angrier by the minute. "Come on, come on Jesus and Mary, where's that carpark?" She asked, as her luck ran out every time. Finally, she took it on herself with no celestial help and let go of her anger. In that moment, her friend walked out of the supermarket and got into her car, leaving Brigid the park next to the front door. As she pulled in to the best carpark in the house, sitting happy, content and smug, she looked up to Heaven and said "Well, yese needn't worry yerselves now, for sure didn't I just find one meself."

The congregation laughed in unison. Spring Equinox was in the air; the thought of new life, long warm days ahead, and the priest in good form, it was enough to warm the cockles of your heart. Ted looked across at Angela and pictured her wailing when they got raided and he wracked his brain to find fifty bottles for the water. There was nothing better than being part of something, no matter how small of a cog in the wheel, to have the Holy Father of the Parish as your trusted confidante and friend was a great honour and guaranteed protection against any foe, large or small. He noticed the Altar Boy at communion, the stature of a boy in the sea of men. His red eyes were sunken deep and black behind dark glasses, his large nose, crooked and swollen. With his jet-black eyebrows and straight dark fringe, he looked even more peculiar than normal, if that was at all possible. He was tolerated and left alone in his position for a reason.

"Why are they laughing, John, why?" Liam asked loudly. They had gotten a lift with Old Jack and were sitting beside him now in the wide seat with the pillars. To get a lift with Jack was a punishment from hell, akin to skydiving with a busted umbrella or sitting passenger on a time trial in the Donegal rally. It was safer to walk, but Jack wouldn't hear of it when there was three empty seats and petrol being burned anyway.

"Murder, git in boys, just git in, in the name of Jayses, we'll be late if yese don't."

Jack tipped his tweed cap and rubbed water from under his left eye, the almost blind eye, although the other eye wasn't much better. He used John as the chief navigator and at least two sections of the Cockhill Bridge wall were John's fault with his wild, stupid and late directions, as he told Jack to turn after he had taken off and the damage done, stones from the bridge wall on the road and splashed into the fast-flowing water. He held the steering wheel at the base, white knuckles facing the sky. His right foot remained permanently planted on the accelerator and, regardless of the clutch, gears, hills, flats or braes, the car was always on a collision course for the nearest heavy object.

Jack had gone off sin for Lent. Weans went off sweets, men went off drink and women went off sex. Jack's sinless ways were easily achieved in Drumfad with no one to bother him or get on his nerves or make noise. In Keelogs, he had broken Lent every day within the first twenty minutes as he gave a roar to the boys and, afterwards, when he thought better of it, steeled his resolve for the next day. He looked to the Heavens for help until at least the end of Lent and put fifty pence in the Trocaire box every time he failed. The box was full.

Even though it was a mortal sin, John didn't go to communion and Liam sat there with him, happily waiting on his choc ice from Cullen's. John watched the Altar Boy amble up like a Holy Joe, and he was happy with his efforts from last night. Although not half as happy as I was. John planned to be in the Backhill by one o'clock and as Saint Patrick's floats made their way up the town street, he would be walking out to Augaweel, free as a bird.

-

Ted loaded the boot of his car with fifty bottles of water. He placed the four bottles of poteen in between and drove to Marian Park in Buncrana, pulling up in the back lane next to the Altar Boy's house. He knocked on the back gate of the house next door, and Seamus McGee lifted the latch. The excitement almost got the better of Ted and he smiled to himself as the curtains from the house next door moved slightly and a dark shadow appeared. He pretended not to notice. Two black eyes watched his every move.

"What's the craic, Ted?" Seamus asked and looked at his watch. He was heading up the town for the parade in ten minutes.

"Have a look at this sur and tell me if ye like it", Ted opened the boot to a colossal amount of poteen, enough to have every man in Inishowen roaring drunk for three days. "I have a supplier in the north, made from the best of good stuff sur, proper malted barley, none of this molasses shite, and a pound less per bottle than Paddy, what do ye think, can ye shift a wheen of bottles for me?" Ted asked and watched as the Altar Boy left the window and crept out into his backyard.

"Here, try one to ye see", he handed Seamus the bottle and he unscrewed the lid. It was like sniffing the finest Irish whiskey, like spring water that had been pressed, condensed, crushed and squeezed into an aromatic overload of barley fields, swaying in the summer breeze, mixed with peat smoke, and magic. The result was a mind-blowing mixture to cure everything from the common cold to rabies and nothing at the same time.

Seamus took a small swig and his joules reddened and warmed instantly.

"That's quare stuff there, Ted. I'll have a few men interested in that gear. Leave me three bottles", he clinked them under his arms and Ted opened the back gate for him.

"Take four Seamus, and the first two are on the house. Ye know where I am when you want more sur and to hell with Paddy, he's had it too good for too long, the cut of him there, and a big head on him, full of chaff." They laughed loudly and over the top, like they had just got hold of their first Playboy magazine and couldn't rightly believe what they were seeing.

"You're the man Ted, on the ball, on the ball, Son of Erin."

Seamus closed the backyard gate with his foot and waved with a nod of his head. The Altar Boy stood glued flat to the backyard wall, happy to be unseen, and relieved that he could get such an easy tout without leaving the comfort of home. It was his lucky day. His bloodshot eyes brightened, and the pain went away temporarily. His mother spoke to him in the loungeroom as if he was still inside and her calling got louder when he didn't answer. Wee Tadhg was the apple of his mothers' eye, and he would make her so proud when he wore the blue uniform. For now, he ran inside to keep her quiet as he watched Seamus hide the bottles in the garden shed and he took down Ted's registration for his employers to cross reference later.

Chapter 13

Dinny was going stir crazy in Augaweel. He trusted Paddy with his life but staying this long in the same place, with combatants able to attack from four sides, went against everything he'd been taught. To move out on his own would put everyone in danger and, unless he could steal a car, the Cortina was a death magnet. He liked to be in control, to position himself with his back against the wall, with a good vantage point, able to see all entrances and exits and count the number of steps to each. He liked to know the gaits of the people in the room, their demeanour, their likelihood of kicking off, of being a tout or a combatant, or a friend, which was something he desperately needed right now. He felt like ploughing through a bottle of Paddy's finest poteen and celebrating the green, white and orange day but that would achieve nothing, and drink was half the reason he was sitting where he was. He placed his face in his hands and warmed himself at the low set gas ring for heating the still.

A dry pine twig snapped about twenty metres in the distance. Dinny dropped to the ground and crawled on all fours to where he could quietly switch off the gas ring. Without the low hiss of the flames, the only constant noise was the light swish of the pines. There was almost complete silence. Dinny cocked the pistol and crawled over to the car, coming to rest against the driver's door, and used the gun barrel as a sight. He scanned slowly around the opening. If he was in the crosshairs of a sniper's rifle, he'd be dead already and wouldn't feel a thing. To be honest, with all the worry and lack of sleep, he almost would have welcomed being put out of his misery. He already knew about John. Paddy had told him last night and he was both looking forward to and dreading it at the same time. Although John was expected, without calling out the code word, he was in danger and the thought of leaving the boy for dead a second time in three days did not bear thinking about. He reminded himself of the plate in his grandmothers' house that said: *strangers are just friends that we haven't met yet* and he imagined shaking John's hand and apologising at the same time.

An orange gas bottle appeared from the direction of the noise and a young man's voice shouted, "who goes there, friend or foe?", as John walked into the clearing. He had neither combat training nor fear. Dinny hugged John like a long-lost son and wept tears of joy. I stood there and hugged them both, their stories would always be entwined and every road in their lives would lead out from this point. It was to be the beginning of a friendship, one that was destined to happen, long before they came here.

-

The Altar Boy made the call, and a closed-door meeting was held at the station. Ted Hagen was lined up to be raided at seven the next morning. Intelligence gathering was a two-way street and the walls of the Buncrana barracks had eyes and ears too. Information looped both ways. The stage was set.

Ian Douglas and Mark May were briefed from both sides of the border, officially and unofficially from their bosses, from handlers and handlers of handlers. There were other operatives in the area, gathering information, listening, keeping an eye, sleeping, trusted, embedded. Ghosts. They watched silently and reported hourly. No detail too small, they watched from the sidelines and waited on the go-ahead for normal rules of engagement — they thrived on rules of engagement.

-

John got back to Keelogs in time for the early news. Liam had had an epileptic seizure in the early afternoon and slept for three hours afterwards. He was still groggy but ran down the lane to meet his brother.

"Where have ye been, John? I've been waiting on ye. Am waiting on the news sur."

Liam hugged his brother tightly around his neck, like he wanted to keep his brother at home, safe and sound. Liam would always be a child in this life, believing in Santa, first one on the bus, first one off the bus, special seat, special plate, special mug, tablets taken inside cream horns, and choc ices from Cullen's, but his soul connection was stronger than anyone's, and he somehow felt the danger and wanted to protect his brother. Without knowing the details, this connection warned John of the sets of eyes on him, and he felt like he was being watched, followed, suddenly a person of interest for all the wrong reasons.

During and after Liam's seizure, for some reason beyond my understanding, he was easier for me to reach, as if talking to him in a dream. He spoke eloquently without the burden of a physical body and his mind was sharp, so sharp that I could hardly believe it was Liam I was talking to. He was here for a reason, his disability for a reason, his life mapped out from his first breath for a reason and, for the most part, his love of John was that reason.

-

Tom and Mick had pulled into an old wallsteads just below Keelogs and sat quietly as the car cooled to the outside temperature and the windows misted. Droplets of cold water ran down the glass. Mick was still put out about being called in today and his opportunity to break Lent like everyone else was drifting away like the last shower that pelted the car with something resembling sleet. He felt like a milk bottle inside a cold and dark fridge, foundered inside this metal and glass container. He could complain but Tom wasn't in the mood for his gurning this evening. Tom opened the report on all things Devenney, anything and everything they knew about us, and pulled on his moustache as his interest sparked.

"Interesting reading on these boys Mick, the old fella was killed in Scotland three years ago, what, in the tunnels I see."

"That's it, Tom, alright, he left them with nothing."

"Nothing? Wasn't there a payout of some sort if he was killed at work?"

"Nah, it was seen as self-inflicted, going against the company safety rules, eye only on the bonus, driller, tunneller, but the word is that they'd gone over the allocated number of men they'd forecast to be killed on that one, and the foreman sided with the company. It wasn't his fault supposedly, a greenhorn drilled into a previous hole from the last blast, drilled into unexploded dets and three of them killed, what a way to go, kaboom!".

"Danger money stamped on the pay packets, and those boys worked hard and played harder, if they had money left over on a Monday, they were getting paid too much or going soft, what."

"It wouldn't surprise me if there's a few more Devenneys in the tunnel locations up and down Britian with dark eyebrows, black skin and gappy teeth", Mick said and put down the window for fresh, cold air. He saw John and Liam on the Keelogs street, getting ready for the news. "What's the story with the young boy, he doesn't look right, like not the full quid", he asked.

"Tadhg told me about him, he could be the Achilles heel for our young fella to talk. We'll give him a few jags at the right time and see if he cries or squeals."

Tom smiled at the thought of provoking John, of getting under his skin and rubbing his nose in the copious amounts of shite that he found himself in. With the young fella only two weeks off being fifteen, if he was going to fight dogged like a man and kick Tadgh when he was down, then he was going to get treated, or mistreated, like one. Friends had to be protected at all costs. With John's older two brothers and two sisters in either England or America, he was a sitting duck, and, in his mind's eye, Tom shot him down, centre of the target. If he hadn't left the house in the next hour, then they'd snavel him on his own street and see how the old mother reacted to having a criminal for a son.

Chapter 14

The ariel was moved and pointed mid-way between Rathmullan and Letterkenny. Liam sat on the chair, waiting, and the nightly crowd appeared as the Queen stood under the ash tree. I sat next to Liam, and Betty took out a chair and sat with her arm around him. She held her youngest child and he felt her earthly love, soul to soul, meant to be, travellers from many lifetimes. Con's death and the drip feed anguish of losing child after child to immigration took its toll on Betty; American and English wakes when they stood at the door, bag packed, sad faced and crying, saying they'd be home when they had some money gathered up. Betty knew that Liam would always be with her, sometimes a hard road, but he would never leave. She remembered the first time she saw him, blue in the face, not crying, not breathing, her screaming, her crying. The nurses that had been so arrogant earlier, quickly rushed him out of the room in a panic. Betty was hysterical. She shouted after them, but not in anger.

"If that wean is going to die, you baptize him, God save my wee baby", she sobbed in the hospital bed.

Waiting on the news, she prayed hard, harder than she had ever prayed and with more meaning. Promises were made. She decreed that however he was taken back, whatever shape, whatever condition, she would love and care for him for her whole life and never once complain. In half an hour, they took Liam back to the room, wrapped up, normal colour and breathing. Like any mother does, she set about loving her youngest child, but deep inside she knew that something wasn't right. But looking at him now, she thought everything was absolutely right, perfect. Betty imagined how her own mother would have loved her, cared for her, protected her from the coldness of the children's home and the anguish that she felt. Holding her babies, she died in the lower room, leaving them to the coldness of the world, with Old Jack, a young man then, standing at the door with her father — broken hearted. She kissed the top of

Liam's head, and he wriggled "Mammy, quet that!" and laughed as he gestured to John to hurry up with the news.

"Two, one, action!" Liam got the news started as the director and pointed at the screen.

"Good evening and welcome to the quarter past five Keelogs news from RTE 1. It's Tuesday 17th of March, Saint Patrick's Day, 1981. Making local news this evening, the low wall on Cockhill bridge has been hit again. Donegal County Council are sending out four men, a digger, a tea hut and a roller man to inspect the damage. It's believed that an old man in a Mark II Escort, with a po called Charlie, was responsible for the damage. He's believed to live somewhere between his thatched house in Drumfad and Keelogs. He is described as six foot two, bandy legged, blind in one eye and can't see out of the other. Anyone that sees this man on the road is advised to jump the ditch and, under no circumstances, accept a lift, unless Liam Devenney is on with him as a guide."

"That's Jack. Hi John, that's Jack sur, sure we were on with him, it was your fault sur. Your directions and all." Liam tried to get his brother's attention through the one-way frequency and laughed at knowing who it was. The newsreader carried on as if he hadn't spoken and the Queen smiled.

"It's Saint Patrick's Day, throw the candle away, that's the word from old Jack, and the long evenings are here again. Buncrana town street was jam packed with lorries and floats today, and the pubs were full of men breaking Lent. They will take both sides of the lane as they come home pure stocious tonight. Liam Devenney also broke Lent today with three packets of toffee and a quarter of bon bons and he'll have sore guts this evening. The only wind we want in the lower room is from the open window.

"In breaking news, every man has to empty the tank before bed and Charlie has only capacity for three small pishes or two big ones, by order of Old Jack.

"In sport, the boys in the Backhill are back practising for tug of war. Any man that has a pair of hob nail boots are needed for the team. Practice is on Tuesday and Thursday evenings, pulling a full forty-four-gallon drum of concrete up and down the pulley. Thin men are needed for the 560 and 640 kilo division. The 720 and catch weight are full and no more heavy anchormen need apply. Last year's effort at the Cockhill sports day was one of the best fights ever against Clonmany. Any man that doesn't train isn't allowed to fight at the sports and that's not negotiable, by order of Martin Quinn.

"And, finally, the man supplying the choc ices to Cullen's shop has died suddenly. There are plenty of the cheaper ice pops in the freezer and all the choc ices have already melted."

"I got one there today, that's not one bit true", Liam chirped, and Betty laughed in the audience.

Liam moved the dial on the TV and sat back down.

"Good evening Ulster, from the car shed at Keelogs. Making news this evening, the hunger strike continues in the Maze. We hope for an end to the whole thing soon.

"The parcel is due from Glasgow any day now, and with only the two of us left, Liam gets to wear all the pink stuff: pink to make the boys wink."

"No way sur", Liam made for the TV and the nightly wrestle began.

"Jesus, now who's this?" Betty stood up as a blue car drove past, slowly. The two occupants looked angry and official and they stared up, more than just an inquisitive survey of the mess and the smoke in the 44-gallon drum, no, they wanted to be intimidating and were happy to put Betty at unease. Not many cars took an interest in Keelogs. Tinkers stopped in occasionally for a drink of fresh water from the bucket, and a man called Tony, selling clothes of all descriptions from the front of his Volkswagen Beetle. The last stranger they saw was the TV licence man, having seen the aerial on display he went looking for the invisible TV, only to find the one in the car shed, wireless, glassless, tubeless and useless.

Tom and Mick had had enough at the wallsteads, frustrated and foundered, and decided to drive up and put an official word on the boy, giving the Devenneys a bit of hurry up. It seemed like a good idea as they approached the white pillars at the foot of the lane. Staring up at the car shed, they saw Betty sitting out in the street with Liam. What they didn't see was myself and the Queen, standing beside each other under the budding ash tree. She held out her hand, and with her palm facing towards the road, repelled them on, without their knowing why. With her there, their dense energy didn't stand a chance of setting foot in Keelogs. John was protected and, while some pain was meant to be, like leaving the permanent reminder above his left eye, unnecessary agitation and strong arming would be dealt with at the highest level: the child of TirConnell would be free to live his life.

The undercover guards went back to the wallsteads and waited. At least the car had a chance to warm up and they left the engine running, blowing warm air, driving out the cold and damp. Dan Dotton had cut a straight stick in the

Planten. It was the usual six feet tall and straight as a rush. He walked with a good step and his yellow coat swished with each Donegal stride, on his way to visit Danny Sheridan and check on the progress of a cow he had treated the week earlier. He approached the wallsteads just below Keelogs and instantly recognised the Garda car and their standout strange plates. His blood boiled and he knew that whoever they were watching or whatever errand they had in the Parish, was going to be no advantage to anyone of any decency.

Tom and Mick saw him approaching and slunk down in their seats, not wanting to engage with the old cow man. He stood at the back of their car and looked in the window. His black hair dropped down over his nose and he smiled a George Devenney smile, one shared by half the old men in the countryside, a sunken face, devoid of teeth, like a madman laughing at the wind, looking at the two Mayo men laying in the Parish, foundered and scunnered on Saint Patrick's Day.

"Hip there boys, hip there", he shouted at the back window. "What's your errand here boys? Do yese know that yese are parked on private land, get on home now? Yese have no errand in the Parish", Dan thumped the boot lid with his fist.

Tom jumped out and ran around to the back of the car, as angry as he had ever been. His eyes bulged like overgrown tadpoles from their sockets.

"Get out of our sight old man, and if you interfere with Garda business again, I'll have you up at the next Law Day, now get on with you, what."

Dan smiled and was happy to have agitated Tom into an angry tirade. Whatever was going on, he would get to the bottom of it and if it meant warning half the countryside, then it was easily done.

-

John left Keelogs when the evening news was over. Liam was happy. John had learnt early from me that there was absolutely no point in worrying about anything because that just attracted it to you. He decided that Liam's seizures weren't a problem and, one day, the cloud would be lifted from his brain, the damage done to him at birth would be rescinded and they'd move to Australia and start again, somewhere with a flushing dunny, running water, sunshine, warm beaches, freedom, girls and no Guards. He looked at the mangled mess of his bicycle behind the pillars and made to walk down the Planting to feed Cissy McGoldrick's cows and put out the dung. Her thatched house backed onto the Queen's dolmen and they were friends, acquaintances, she was one of the few people to have seen her. It was the centre of solace for John, and no matter what was happening, old Cissy always seemed to have the right question and answer as she looked into the coals of the open fire, beyond the crane and the black pots hanging over them.

It was near on dark, and the light faded quickly as a squally shower left Rathmullan and headed across to visit the Parish. He turned down Carolina Road and looked into the field where small black rabbits sheltered, two feet from the nearest whun bushes. He was almost at the wallsteads when he saw the car parked off the road, he knew who they were.

Tom got out and unzipped his leather jacket, ready for action. John stopped and decided to run back up the road but ran straight into the large frame of Ass's Teeth. Mick put John's right arm in a lock behind his back and lifted his wrist into the pain threshold when he wanted him to move.

"Walk down to the car, young Devenney and don't give us trouble or ye'll feel it", Mick said with great authority, breathing deathly fumes into the back of John's head. John was put into the back seat and Mick sat there with him. Tom drove and they headed down towards Stragill shore, slowly making their way through the Planting. The Queen watched and followed from a distance; John wasn't on his own.

"Give us your name", Mick said, as he fixed himself comfortably in the back seat. "Well, come on, give us your full name."

John smiled out the window at the trees and branches overhanging the road, meeting in the middle, soon to be a full canopy and cocoon of leaves and life. He had no fear of these men. They meant nothing and, at best, he'd feel physical pain which meant less than nothing to him. He laughed out loud and Mick glanced a punch on his shoulder, hard, heavy and weighted but glancing. Next one would be harder.

He asked again, but this time Mick shouted at him from the front, "Give us your name, or we'll take you up to your wee mammy and that useless disabled brother of yours, then you'll give it, what".

John smiled at the question, and he thought on the story from the potato field last year, when James Toland was fighting at the taxi rank in Acton High Street in London, after being at the Irish club. They rolled around on the pavement, half hitting, half slapping each other, and the Police were called. When they arrived, the fight was over and they both looked down the street, as if it was someone else. The policeman said to James; "give me your name".

James responded, “If I give you my name, what name will I use myself sur?”, and that was the end of the conversation as the two boys got in the taxi and away home.

Chapter 15

"Am I saying something amusing to you Devenney? I'll put the smile off you damn quick now, do you hear me. Answer me or we'll take this to the station." Mick goaded John and hit him again while Tom remained quiet in the front, watching him intently in the mirror, with a face like a slapped arse.

"My name is John Gerald Devenney", he replied, quietly, with reverence, as if he was talking to two priests in the confessional.

"Well John, we're getting somewhere now, what", Tom spoke into the mirror. "We hear you've been a bad boy, interfering with people on official Garda business, assault and battery, what?" Tom spoke down to his captive in the back.

John was aware of the pull that the Altar Boy had at the Buncrana station. Without his eyes and ears, outsider Guards could only mop up after an incident or hear about it three months after the event.

"I don't know what you're talking about, sur", John replied, and Mick angled himself to get a hold of John's shoulder and squeeze it hard, like he was imparting knowledge through the laying on of hands, right deep into him, like I used to hold a young fella's arm with the thran Devenney grip, to somehow magically impart knowledge through pain. John looked the Guard in the eyes, he felt nothing and gave away nothing. Tom pulled the car up by the caravans on Stragill shore. Seagulls walked along the rippled sand; their tail feathers ruffled in the wind. It was near on dark, and the pure whites of the birds illuminated the greyness and dark skies like streetlamps scattered on the strand. John felt claustrophobic in the back seat and unable to straighten his legs or move his knees, like someone had placed a bag on his head, like he was drowning in a tight space, no room to move, no room to breathe, and dealing with a pair of bastards from hell itself. He remembered being one of thirteen under thirteens, on the way to a football game in Carn, all jammed into a Talbot sunbeam, and he, squeezed between two others, and feeling the lid of the glass hatchback touching his nose, watching the road disappear, stuck and sweating. He vowed to never play another game. The Queen stood outside the car and felt his panic. She showed the palms of her hands to the Guards again and Mick released his grip and Tom, for no particular reason, decided to walk John along the shoreline, Guard on either side.

"Let's get out and walk here", Tom said, "we're getting nowhere," thinking to try a different tack.

"Let me tell you what we know, and you can fill in the blanks, are you with me John Gerald? What". They walked into the Donegal dusk while the red light of the buoy between Rathmullan and Stragill gave off an intermittent danger signal that the Guards were at the shore.

"You are keeping bad company with an ex-convict in the Backhill and we had surveillance on you. You assaulted the Garda operative and now battery charges have been laid against you, are you with me, what? I can get you sent away for a while, young offenders, doesn't look good for you, and the state of the house up there and your brother can't cross the road on his own or tie his own shoelaces, useless, what."

Tom was unapologetic in his assessment of John's life, like it was his fault for being born there. His start in life couldn't have been further from the truth. John had picked the start, the location, the people and, above all, Tom and Mick, to steel his resolve, to learn, and most of all, to *feel* life, not just look at it and let it pass, but feel it deep within his soul, drinking in the knowledge gained and hopefully not needing to come back again, enlightened, free.

Deep, hard, strong and unquenched Devenney fury ran through John's mind, as countless centuries of colonialism, guagers, landlords, middlemen, customs and excise officers rose to the surface through his Inishowen and TirConnell DNA. John's face remained expressionless, and he carefully thought about what was said. Any stress on his mother, any bother coming to the door, on top of everything else, would send her to the mental asylum in Letterkenny, she'd be picked up in a plain white van with men in white coats and syringes full of Valium. He decided then and there, as the words from his father about taking your dealer's trick rang in his ear, that being in control and the chance of a fair day's pay for a hard day's work was next to nothing; whatever had to be done, would be done, and he'd walk the tightrope between law and order, friend and foe, without hurting a soul.

"Assault? I have assaulted no one", John replied, "anyway, whoever came at me was up for a fight, but you know that already, don't you, Tom?"

"Don't get too forward with us now, boy, its Guard to you. I see from the cut over your eye that you've been talking when you should have been listening", Mick said and stepped over a large jellyfish, laying cold and wet in the ripples, waiting for the far-out tide to come back in, to float it away, dead or alive, into the North Atlantic.

"What were you doing at Paddy Ennis' house? It's your last chance before we charge you, what", Tom asked as they stopped by the water's edge, three dark silhouettes against the cold milky light of the setting sun and the relentless soft lapping of the small waves on the strand.

John knew they weren't talking in an official capacity, or they'd be in the barracks already, with old, grey, hard looking senior Guards breathing down his neck, intimidating him with their accents, their stripes, their authority and their brylcreme combovers.

The Queen walked between them, and she spoke to John as I trailed along behind.

"I was out with Paddy talking about my father, if you have any interest in that?" John started, being surprised at his own calmness.

"Go on", Tom replied.

"They were in Scotland together, as young fellas, tatty hoking, bumming from one place to another, starving until they got work knocking in pegs on sleepers in the railway for two pound a day. I wanted to know more, to find out what my father was like, what kind of a man he was, you know what I mean sur?" he looked at both his captors in turn, trying to reason with them.

"I think you're lying through your teeth, boy, but when we get something on you the charges will stick, and a charge in Donegal at your age will come back to bite you when you're looking for a green card for the good old USofA to be with your brothers."

Mick was angry, annoyed at the end of a long day and to hell with poverty, he laid it on thick and wanted to duck him under the waves until he talked.

"Let's take him to the barracks now Tom, and give him a couple of nights in the cell and a bit of a belting with the yellow pages, what do ye think?" He looked across at his mate and winked, an old fashioned, goat herder's wink, having feigned a yawn and a donkey's neigh in his excitement.

"If you help us John, we can help you, we're your best friends to have amongst these blackguards. Look at the state of you, what, you look like no one owns you." Tom made a last ditch offer as they headed back to the car.

"You're young and impressionable, and you're moving in circles that will either get you killed or a lifetime of jail, or both. I'll see if the charges can be dropped but you're on your first and final warning, what, and you can find your own way home I'm sure."

Tom left his closing argument there for John to consider. The pair crouched their large frames into the car and took off into the darkness. They kept the lights off until well up past the warren, none the wiser for their interrogation, although it made sense to Tom that Tadhg made the first move against the boy. John seemed genuine, truthful, and he had a warmth to his personality that was way beyond his years that Tom liked instantly. He seemed feisty and confident, but, most of all, he displayed no fear from anything on two feet and very little on four, and it concerned him what young Devenney would be capable of in the next wheen of years. He was sure of one thing, their paths would meet again, and soon.

John made it to Cissy McGoldrick's with the only visible light being the caged outside light above the lower room window, under the thatch, giving a weak, almost cold glow to the mucky, cobbled street and casting dark shadows along the rough whitewashed walls. There was a light on in the black pitch-roofed byre and barn accompanied by a sweet, not offensive, smell of cow dung, newborn calves, bedding straw and fresh hay. Cissy appeared out of the byre illuminated by a brattle of hay in her arms, none too happy with the lateness of the help. Her face was winter red and ruddy, it spoke of cold wind, frosty mornings and windswept evenings, and she looked forward to summer more than anyone. Wearing two pairs of socks, plastic bags for leaks, wellingtons, trousers, three jumpers and a dress over everything, she dropped the hay in the manger and laughed into her hands. Late or not, it was always great to see John and he brightened her street more than any electrical lamp ever could. Her house was a place of solace, of deafening quiet and John could think here, take stock, and decide which road to go down. Even the rain knew that falling heavy on her roof made no difference as the thatch quietly protected the occupant and allowed the house to breathe, as well as the people within it.

Cissy poured part boiling water from the black kettle and wet the tea. She boiled two eggs on the side of the coals in a black bean tin and fixed the fire from a low glow to dancing flames with a wheen of whun bush branches. John finished off outside and ducked his head at the front door, taking his spot at the top of the table, looking out the small window to the street and the world beyond.

"Tell me the truth John, what happened your face?" She asked, still looking into the fire, concentrating on the flames, not wanting to look at the cut of his left eye.

"I tripped going up the Planten and hit my head on a stone", he replied.

"Aye, deed it happened ye in the Planten, but it was no trip", she didn't push the question any further, but she knew the Queen well, and some people even said she *was* the Queen in the dense frequency we could see. She looked at John and smiled, then began to laugh at the stupidity of asking a question that she already knew the answer to. Her eyes lit up like whun bushes on fire and she put her face into her cupped hands and laughed hysterically.

"John Devenney, you are clean cracked!"

The events of the past week lay in front of my grandson and, under the protection of the thatched roof, tea and boiled eggs, he took stock, and laughed into his hands as well — it was catching.

Chapter 16

Ted slept with one eye open. Every time tiredness took him to another place, his anxiety and fast beating heart brought him back to reality and fully awake, as a lone bird in the distance hooted softly, like a ship's horn, keeping him company. A solitary car drove past the house around six o'clock, just as the day was waking up. It was either the Holy Father's man or a Guard, but it definitely wasn't local. He felt like getting up and leaving the front door open, but nothing could be obvious, everything normal, run of the mill, ready for the surprise.

At ten past seven, three carloads pulled up on Ted's street and the loud knock came at the door. Ted answered and received the search warrant; he was informed loudly, like a nurse speaking to a deaf patient with Alzheimer's, that they had due cause to search every part of his property, outhouses and sheds. Angela screamed at Ted, blindsided, what the hell had he done this time? By half past seven, the house was alive with the sounds and mayhem of thirteen weans from eighteen to a newborn. Fourteen Guards searched the house inside out, upside down and every drawer, cupboard and shelf until everything had been checked.

Finally, an excited pitched yell came from the main bedroom, "I have something here, two clear bottles, well hidden under the bed", the young Guard took the bottles up to the kitchen and the boss opened them, excited to finally have the evidence. He sniffed both bottles and it was either water or the blandest poteen that had ever graced Inishowen. He poured some into the sink.

"What have we here, Mr O'Hagen?" he asked.

"It's Hagen, no need for the O", Ted replied. "I believe that's two bottles of holy water from Angela's pilgrimage to Knock last year. You're welcome to bless your crew for the coming year with it if ye want."

Ted smiled and surveyed the house. It reminded him of Cissy McGoldrick's thatched house, everything on the floor, every surface full, drawers laying open, chockers, spilling out, but she knew exactly where everything was, could put her hand on it, dosing bottles, sweets, calf milk replacer, cudding cake, holy water, matches and layers mash for the hens. Ted looked across at his wife as she cursed the Guards black and blue, she looked beautiful every day but even more so in her anger. It would take some sweet talking and smooching to get back into her good books, and a lot more besides to get some action back in the thresher. It felt like the end of the baby train. He smiled at the thought that he had probably had enough at thirteen weans, and she caught his eye. She was sharp as a pointy pencil, and he needn't come around here a drinkin' with a lovin' on his mind. He got the message, loud and clear.

"Stay where you are Mr O'Hagen, we're not done here yet by a long shot."

The Sargeant was angry as a bag of cats and his face reddened instantly as a rush of adrenaline zapped him, giving him the strength to kill a man with his bare hands and silencing this annoying smart arse. He felt like taking the man of the house outside and beating his knees with a baton, in front of his brood, until he crawled on all fours where he belonged. In his mind's eye, Ted begged for mercy and gave up his stash of poteen, and everyone got their photo taken for the front page of Friday's Derry Journal and they all went home happy.

Ted smiled inwardly and knew that it was only quarter to eight and he needed to keep them at the house for as long as possible. He looked out towards the byre and barn, as if keeping them away from there, and they followed the scent like bloodhounds on a hunt with gentry in red coats and white trousers. Ted thought about mentioning the O again in Hagen but, like any good raid, they would yield something and the less antagonistic he was from here on, the better it would be in the long run. Whatever Peter Mulligan was doing, he needed to be quick. Everything was in close proximity here and Dinny was already on the move, less than a mile as the crow flies.

-

Leo Miller checked the coin slot at the public telephone box in Linsfort after every user. The twenty pence pieces, and particularly the fifties, had a way of getting stuck and a delayed reaction when the receiver was replaced yielded more money than Mickey Carey's slot machines and never cost him a penny in outlay. Leo stood permanently at the fingerpost, next to the post office that was once a British army barracks. He moved occasionally to drive his two cows on the long acre but generally only on summer evenings and mild days. The grass was dead where he stood in all weathers and his track to and from the phone box resembled a rabbits' path in a warren, smooth, worn and anything but straight. The three carloads of Guards ignored Leo. Some of them had been on patrol out this way and he was known to them as kooky and a simpleton but basically harmless. Mark O'Malley, in the second car, laughed at the cut of him, standing in his brown suit, shiny and blackened from years of wear, his black curly hair and his dark, gypsy face with eyes that followed you, without turning his head.

"The height of Donegal fashion week, ladies and gentlemen, may I present Leo Miller, a man that can be looking at a shooting star and finding tuppence on the road at the same time."

Mark cracked himself up and everyone was in the best of form. There was nothing like a good old raid to get the day started, not to mention the pouring of perfectly good poteen into a farmer's dung midden. It didn't get any better and surely beat pulling van loads of workers over at the steel bridge for doing ten over the speed limit. With lunch provided in The Town Clock afterwards, courtesy of the State, it was worth the cost of the stamp to write home to Mayo about.

Leo went straight to the phone after he observed the cars and called Peter at home. He spoke in a low tone, as he didn't possess a high one and, although quiet in his delivery, he was animated and excited to be part of the Holy Father's plan. He knew the number plates, how many occupants in each car and placed great emphasis on the lead car, passenger side, Tiny Tony.

Tony was a fresh-faced recruit when he first came to the town. He had a big frame, like a sycamore tree in early spring, potentially huge but bare of vegetation until fattened by sun and rain and leaves. Tony had the kind of frame that with the right amount of nourishment from Tommy's chip shop and Flaherty's Guinness, filled out to be a great sized man altogether. The springs on the left-hand side of the car were low and they groaned and squeaked at each and every pothole. He was the senior sergeant on the raid, the man in charge, and if there was one thing he hated more than being hungry, it was being caught out with dud intel. He wasn't sure about this run to the Parish and something was telling him that the Altar Boy had shit the nest this time. Gut feeling. He looked down at his belly, gaping pink and hairy between the buttons of his shirt and decided not to use that phrase again, even when talking to himself.

"One more thing, Peter," Leo looked around and stepped outside the box for a moment to check for listeners, as if the first lot of information wasn't important.

"Jayses, Leo, what, in under Jesus, hurry up Leo, for fuck's sake", Peter was agitated, desperate to get going.

"The Guards are at Ted's place, but I saw a Northern yok, just after six o'clock this morning, driving past slowly sur, I think they know all about this. Watch yerself th'day sur." Leo whispered loudly into the receiver with the steam of his breath sitting on the mouthpiece like water on black oil.

"Make, registration, men?" Peter asked quick fire, military style, like a spray from a machine gun.

"Red two litre Capri, AUI 717, three of them. Never saw them before in all their runs to the Parish, they're cleanskins, new men, Peter, fresh. Ghosts, Peter, Ghosts." Leo memorised faces, names and number plates in that order. Every car that went past, every tractor, motorbike or bicycle, Leo could recount them in great detail, three weeks later. Leo was uneasy about what he saw, and the three men were a hit squad if ever he saw one.

"Whatever ye have planned th'day Peter, cancel it and lay low", Leo pleaded as the feeling of doom took hold. He was susceptible to premonitions and lived somewhere between dense earthly reality and the outer world, where everything was known. As he again looked at the men in his mind's eye, he could see and feel and smell death. He was rarely wrong. Ian Douglas and Mark May were marked men in the Free State now, but they knew this area well, had stayed in caravans at Stragill shore and Claggan Brae for weeks before flushing out Dinny originally.

Dead men carry no tales their commanding Officer screamed at them following their last attempt in Buncrana, and *how could they start such a public chase and then let him get away? If they were policemen, they'd have been giving out parking tickets for a month.* They had briefed the next crew on the lay of the land. It was anyone's guess, including my own, if they would make an appearance today as well.

"Good man Leo, we have no choice today. Go back to the fingerpost and ring again as soon as they all leave there, and, Leo, if there's anybody in the phone box at that time, bounce them out with a kick in the arse, got it?"

"Aye Peter, that'll be no bother."

Leo hung up the phone and looked at his small frame and thin arms in the small panes of glass and multiple times in the cracked sections; he hoped there wasn't a farmer with big hands and a bad attitude calling for the vet or the Artificial Insemination man when the time came. He was a reconnaissance man, intel under the guise of an idiot and left the fighting to someone else. He checked the refund chute for money. Force of habit.

-

At ten to eight, the first of the Guards' cars turned at the fingerpost towards Buncrana. The young Guard came to a full stop at the intersection and Tiny rolled his eyes, as if there was any need out here. He looked across at Leo and thought better of his impatience, asking the young recruit to pull in beside the mute and rolled down the window. He was annoyed at the result of the morning, the inconvenience, the red-faced shame amongst his peers, and the thought of the farmers laughing in their potato fields as they sowed the year's crop was almost too much to bear. A mere small fine for an out-of-date shotgun licence didn't seem like a fair compensation for the efforts they went to with Ted.

"You there, I say you there, I want to have a word with you", Tony spoke to the side of Leo's face. His body filled the full front passenger seat and half the back seat as well.

"Can you hear me? I'm talking to you sir, have you seen any strange activity down this way?" Tiny asked again, more frustration and anger being added to the already wasted morning.

Leo looked over the hedge with his back to him, into the green field of rushes and whun bushes and beyond to the other side of the water as the mirror of calm water in the Swilly caught the reflection of the mountains on the other side. Leo thought it looked like a picture, framed just for him. He lit a cigarette and took a drag, the smoke drifting over the hedge like a white thought. He stared at the red glow and smoked the rest of the fag with his eyes, totally oblivious to the car parked beside him. He smiled on the inside. Tony gestured for the driver to carry on and was sorry he stopped at all, making him angrier than he already was, if that was possible. He muttered under his heavy breath that he'd need something one day and then see how he likes it, bloody weirdo.

The second and third car followed about an hour later, as the crew searched the outhouses and ditches around Ted's place. Leo skipped quickly to the phone box with his pocket full of recycled Telecom coins.

"They've all gone now in the past five minutes, all heading back to the town. Tiny left at ten to eight, and he's on the war path."

He was happy to have done a good turn for Peter, and he pictured himself enjoying a wheen of pints by the fire in the next week or two, without having to dip into his Telecom money. He spoke to himself, whispering the words, agreeing with himself, and laughing, like a lunatic, although he was anything but.

"You there, I say you there, I want to have a word", he whispered with the accent as he held up the fingerpost and lit another smoke. He felt like Denis Thatcher, thought of as a handbag holder, an imbecile, and probably somewhere in his past, a fingerpost man himself. He maintained that it was better to say nothing and be thought a fool, than to open one's mouth and remove all doubt. It was probably the only thing that Leo and Denis would agree on. It had been a great morning altogether. Wild Craic.

Chapter 17

Dinny slept with the gun under his pillow, if you could call it sleep. It morphed somewhere between worry and wishful thinking that he was already out of the poteen den and in a proper safe house. When he did drop off, his eyes moved rapidly under their closed lids and battles were fought, hostages were taken, interrogations, executions. The faces of his enemies and his friends, some dead, some alive, invaded his sleep and would do so until he met them again when he took his last breath. That moment felt close and although he was not a spiritual man or in any way religious, apart from being a Catholic republican, he said a few Hail Marys and rushed over the part at the end as he dare not think about *now and at the hour of our death, Amen.* His feet twitched and ran, like an overtired dog sleeping in front of the fire, chasing rabbits and fighting at the last dog concert where the strongest male got the girl. Paddy had given him sparse details about how the Guards would be made busy, but Dinny knew better than anyone that no matter how strong the chain was, how trusted your inner circle was, one rotten cog, one informer, one turned volunteer, could bring the whole thing undone. He woke as the tarp flapped between the pine trees, and he huddled into the sleeping blanket for hopefully his last night in the den, maybe his last night on earth.

Paddy Poteen got out to the den before the first awakening of the dawn. He kept the lights off in the house and moved around silently, as if screws or Guards were listening. He used the experience of being in jail to his advantage in every situation on the outside. He opened the back window and climbed out like he was just after robbing his own place. His shoes were black, soft and light to tread. The dim light of the waxing moon lit the way, and he took one of four different paths through the heather. It brushed against his legs and the purple flowers acted like guideposts, softly illuminated by the weak moon. Getting caught with a wee still in Inishowen was an institution, a badge of honour against conformity, a tradition dating back three hundred years and even a good advertisement to the public - Friday's Derry Journal story mostly meant increased sales after a conviction - but it was an entirely different ball game if Dinny was found out here.

A win for the Irish Free State or a win for the Crown mattered little in this part of Donegal. It was an isolated patch that was ignored by Dublin and held the disdain of Belfast and London. The partition map of 1922 cared little for the country and the people, and even less for the trouble created by having a border. It was, however, a close escape route for men like Dinny. The ensuing bitter Irish civil war between pro and anti-treaty with Britain was still felt here, as if yesterday, or an hour ago, timeless, almost like my side of the fence now. It made no difference, as this generation struggled to wake up from the past and, in doing so, kicked an angry, mean dog from its sleep, only to wonder why it would turn around and bite them. Every man lifted or killed was seen as a suppression of the insurrection, a final clean-up of anti-treaty men, an end to the uprising and an acceptance of the colonial status quo that London ruled their western neighbours, all thirty-two counties.

Regardless of what he'd done in the past or the events that led him to walk out over the hill that night, Paddy was free of the everyday worries, he felt selfless, empowered to be doing something other than for money or mere personal gain. He felt like his spirit had been granted freedom from the mundane and, as he looked across the dark countryside, lightless, lifeless, normal working people, farmers, all asleep, he wondered how many other mad bastards besides himself and the Holy Father would be doing this. How many others, with full bellies of meat, peas and potato poundies and Coronation Street on the TV would even care.

-

Betty had an alarm clock in the upper room. It stood in an overturned saucepan for maximum noise, facing the bed and far enough away to make her get out to stop the racket. It was used sparingly and there was nothing worse than having her dreams disturbed by a mechanical bell. It reminded her of a cold, stale smelling orphanage, somewhere in the forgotten past, the sound of order, rigour, rows of beds and crying weans. It was never needed in the lower room. John set his alarm in his mind's eye at ten past eleven and pushed in against his brother, settling into the comfortable spot between the springs and stuffing in the mattress. Old Jack was warming up in the brighter evenings and his white feet poked out the bottom of the blankets, while his long johns rode up his bony, spindly shins. Even without the fire on, there was little need of the green army coat over the top of the blankets now and John threw it off onto the timber floorboards. The cold metal buttons dropped heavily, like tuppences rushing into the metal chutes from the one arm bandits in Carey's. He thought of the soldier that originally wore the coat and which side he fought for. It made no difference to him. John refused to worry but, every so often, white butterflies tapped on the back of his heart at the thought of tomorrow morning, and his instructions from Paddy. He glanced once more at his Timex watch on the worn black leather strap, his most prized possession that his eldest brother left him before going to San Francisco. He shut his eyes, saying to his subconscious mind *quarter to six*: his clock was set.

-

Any time before half past seven was the middle of the night in Keelogs. John quietly turned the round handle of the lower room door and walked gently around the mouse hole, avoiding the squeaky boards. Liam turned over for a second sleep and fell directly into the warm spot left by his brother. Charlie the po was full of piddle and spits on the side of the hearth and Old Jack lay in the foetal position, his white feet disappeared up under the blankets in the cool of the morning. The old man's dreams took him to the thatched house, and every single stalk of rye was the most beautiful woman he had ever seen. They all loved Jack and Jack only. He basked in the glorious dream and being the centre of attention again, *the good gossoon,* the charming eligible bachelor, and he had to pick one to begin with. He carried her over the flagstone threshold in Drumfad as the lower room door clicked shut. It was still the middle of the night, and he looked forward to the next two hours of pure passion and not a Rosary bead in sight. So much thatch, so many women, so little time.

John opened the kitchen door and the black clocks scurried behind the range, twenty, thirty, from all over the floor, and within seconds they were gone into the gap behind the oven, non-existent in the daylight hours and back to the warmth of the country hearth. Even the clocks considered six o'clock an ungodly hour in Keelogs. He stoked the ashes and threw a wheen of black clods of turf on top. It smoked instantly and faint red flames started up. He sat there for a while, looking into the fire and thought about pulling up his trouser legs and lighting a smoke, like old Con would do. Today was an auspicious day. He was a boy in the company of men, hardened men, and they were playing for keeps. Men might live or die on how he performed today. As always, he refused to worry. He felt the presence of the Queen and the fairies behind, in front and all around him. Jesus looked down from the sacred heart picture, partly obscured by the clothes from the pulley line. He cast a lonely figure from above the red light, almost black from years of smoke, his open hands sent love and protection for the day. I stood there beside him and was glad of the assistance for my grandson. He would need every bit of it.

John walked out over Drumfad and kept off the road. Even though it was as lonely a road as Ireland possessed, it had accessways, gaps, laneways, ditches and hedges for a man to launch a surprise attack. The experience with the Altar Boy was fresh in his mind and although he relished meeting him again and continuing where he left off, it was the ghosts, and especially ghosts with guns, that had him spooked, and for good reason. Any chance of being followed was a dropping of breadcrumbs for the enemy. He thought about his father on the walk out over the hill. He had been flooding his thoughts since he woke and he tried to picture his face, his expression, the clearing of his dusty and tobacco coated throat and his reservations about getting involved with men like Paddy, Dinny and the Holy Father.

As John squelched through the soft, wet fields, making ground slowly towards the standing stone at the top of Drumfad, he listened as his father came through in the early morning mist, six weeks before May Day, when fairies could be seen at first light and the veil between the worlds was lifted in the mystical dawn.

It's like this sur, all youse gents, aye, you included, young and all as you are, are playing a dangerous game, against men that kill for the craic, to have another number on their wall, to look at, to boast about, to write a book one day when they have all their killing done for Queen and country.

Con cleared his throat again and spoke with vigour, like he was on a long-distance call and only had enough money to tell the important things. Words like I love you, I miss you and apologies for not being there when needed would need to wait for the next call, if there was to be a next call, if John made it through the day at all.

Con had said nothing since his death. He had moved on quickly, leaving his earthly family to it, as he walked into the light after the explosion and didn't look back. It was a shock. One minute drilling, loud, wet and hot, and the next, an almighty flash and a ferocious blast lifting and hurling him through the darkness like lead pellets from a shotgun. There was instant pain and then nothing. He watched it unfold like it was happening to someone else. He left the mangled body under the rubble and got out of there quickly, homeward bound and glad to get away as the light descended and the familiar faces of his ancestors, my father and mother, angels, friends, enemies and soulmates helped his crossing. Although it may have seemed like a wasted journey to some on earth, it was the most important role he had ever played and the boy walking through the hill would have learnt nothing if mollycoddled in cotton wool and spoilt with choc ices and bottles of lemonade mineral, sitting cross-eyed watching television and scratching himself. Today was one of the few days he would appear, and it took a very special occasion to make it happen.

John and Con both looked across at Old Jack's thatched house in Drumfad at the same time. They too saw the beautiful women adorning the roof and heard the commotion in the lower room as Jack carried Sally Anne onto the steel framed bed. He lit a match to the twigs that the crow had dropped down the chimney and the room became warm and cosy in an instant, the whitewashed walls reflecting the ochre, orange and red of the bird's labour. Their shadows from the dancing flames made love on the ceiling, warm and tender like there was no tomorrow, no today and no yesterday either, just that moment. With the roller blinds down and the doors closed to the outside world, the house and contents, including the vessels on the dresser, shook with the excitement of young love until Jack would wake in Keelogs and break the spell. Con let out his usual "*Humph*" and although John couldn't see him, they both looked away at the same time and laughed.

I have one last piece of advice for ye, John, for I can see ye wont back away from this. Watch yer left flank th'day. Ye'll be in the crosshairs of military men, trained men, trained killers. Whatever you do, don't let me be speaking to you face to face this evening. And one more thing, you're a proud son of Erin and don't let holy men tell you that pride is a sin. That's rubbish. Ego and pride are what makes poor men good and good men great. Without it, ye might as well accept yer fate when yer born and put in yer time, like a marked man on death row having no control of his own life and doing what he's told. Stand tall, be proud, whatever it takes, mind this, whatever it takes, do ye hear me sur? I'm away now, on the ball sur, on the ball, don't let me see you any time soon son.

"Whatever it takes", John answered his father and all the beings around him. Even though he felt alone on the walk, all but for the familiar sound of his father, he was anything but. He had never thought on pride or what it meant. Devenney pride was being able to roll down a fertiliser bag and gather potatoes like a man and get paid like one, but walking up for communion on a Sunday morning with the toes out of his shoes didn't bother him either. Maybe it was more important on the other side, but he'd think on it this evening after the news, after everything had gone well.

The Altar Boy was with him in spirit. Connected to John by long, thick, wiry, straw-like cords of attachment. John felt his presence, his anger and meanness of spirit. He felt their feuding in past lifetimes, unresolved differences, and he made a conscious decision to end it this time, one way or another. He shook off the thoughts of his nemesis like dry soot falling into the fireplace for a chimney sweep. The black dust rose and made its way into the bright blue sky, dissipating out to join the infinite dust of time and space. He knew that the raid on Ted's place would be make or break for Tadhg and it was only a matter of time before he'd have to leave the security of his mother's apron and move away, because *he* was the marked man now. The words of his father echoed through his thoughts as he entered the edge of the pine forest in Augaweel and looked forward to the theatre. In the stillness of the morning, a two-way was activated.

"Second man entering from the western side."

Chapter 18

John made it to the den at half past six and waited at the edge of the clearing, casing out the spot before entering, making sure he wasn't compromised. I watched the other entrance and could see the eyes on him. Although I couldn't warn him, I knew the Queen wouldn't be far away if and when the play got up, unless it was his time, and, if that was the case, well, the perfect scene in the valley of tears had been set. It was a definite exit point.

Paddy used the gas burner to boil tea and the still was as cold as an assassin's heart. The escape of the gas, the flutter of the flames and the gentle boiling of the water gave the morning normality, just another day in Augaweel. Paddy signalled John to come in and they waited on the news from Peter. The aroma of fresh, black, plumping tea in the kettle overtook the stale sweet alcohol smell of poteen. Waiting, nervous waiting, was worse than being in the fight itself for Dinny. If everything went to plan and a great number of Guards were taken out of circulation, he'd be moved to a permanent safehouse by ten o'clock.

The plan was simple, and Paddy went over it one more time.

"We get into position by seven o'clock and at no time come back here", he was reminding himself as much as he was giving instructions.

"John, you make your way to the lookout and watch the main road. When Peter turns up, give me the signal on channel 27 and say no more."

Paddy was on edge, almost hyperactive, picking up his cup, forgetting to drink, leaving it down, distracted and then not be able to find it again. He caught himself, took a wheen of deep breaths and remembered what his cellmate told him in Mountjoy: *If I'm panicked and stressed, and I'm the boss, then every man for a hundred yards will follow suit, so quit yer stressin' and be calm from the teeth out, relax and laugh it off.*

Paddy calmed himself and took a whole new tack.

“Did ever I tell yese about the best custard in Ireland?” Paddy asked with a smile, as if he’d just lined up three fresh pints of cold beer and was ready to tell a yarn.

“I don’t think you have”, John replied, and he looked forward to talking about anything else but what was in front of him.

“Two years ago, I had a five hundred pound fine from Buncrana courthouse and the same from Carndonagh from a raid at the house and I was caught selling in Carn. They got nothin’ worth, but enough for them to take me to the next Law Day. The judge asked me *how do you plead? mister Ennis*, and says I, is this a fifty- fifty question your honour, or do a have a choice in the matter?”

“No”, he replied, “you do not. You continue to flaunt the law by making illegal and sometimes dangerous quantities of poteen. Five hundred pound fine. Dismissed.”

“That was alright, and it was the same story in Carn. I got my name in the Derry Journal twice in a fortnight. I was run aff my feet making poteen for a month afterwards and had more money than I knew what to do with. The Guards came out three or four times with the demand for the fine, and at the rear they’d had enough and said there’s nothing more for ye than a run to Mountjoy for a month to pay it aff.

“Says I, ’that’s no bother, come any day ye like’ and I had the bag packed and ready, down in the room. They came out in a taxi one Monday morning and lifted me and I sat in the back, between two big Guards on either side of me. We drove all the way to Dublin in an old Wolsleley 1660 and it was the best day’s craic. We couldn’t drive through the North and kept to the free-state roads, so we drove through Sligo, great feed at Carrick on Shannon, Mullingar and Dublin. I was like a wean going on my holidays, even the Guards enjoyed it.”

Dinny had lit a smoke, and as the poteen man was rambling, his drone and sense of calm finally lifted the tension from his shoulders. John had a smile from ear to ear and cared for nothing, he nudged Paddy to go on with the story, thinking that some of this material could be used in the nightly news.

“Anyway, we arrived in the Joy, not my first rodeo there by any stretch, and the Guards escorted me in and the warden took my details and all, again. I knew him well. He said ’what are you here for Paddy. I mean, what did you do this time?’

"I said, 'making wee still, ye know sur, a bit of poteen sur, only a wheen of bottles here and there, ye know.'

"He said, 'well Paddy, that's more of a community service than a crime in my book, and I have good news for you and bad news for you.'

"'Tell me the good news first', says I.

"'We have no room for you here, so we're sending you back home in the taxi again.'

"'What, five fucken hours? Jesus Mary and Joseph, I'll be jetlagged by the time I get home. What's the bad news?'

"No custard, you've missed the dinner."

John laughed as freely as Liam at the nightly news. He liked the poteen man, despite the warnings from his father. He was a rogue, a good rogue, while there was not exactly honour amongst thieves, there was honour in belonging, and whether it was the wrong side of the fence, depended on who was asking the question and how silver the spoon was that was sticking out of their mouth. He had a pack of cards in front of him, shuffled, worn and tatty, but still a full pack and he intended to play them, every last one, until he found the queen of hearts. He was glad of the distraction, and he realised that Paddy possessed a rare gift, the rare ability to make people laugh and forget their troubles, like Betty going to see Doctor Mclaughlin with a great medical worry, only to forget what she came in for when he made her laugh for ten minutes. John hoped to never forget this, and I can tell you that he never did.

John was to stay hidden for the most part during the lift and shift, a trusted set of eyes and ears, but at no time was he to enter harm's way, whatever was happening, the young fella had to be kept safe. Paddy owed it to Con, and for some strange reason he could taste the raw turnips that they stole in Scotland; for the first time since his death, he felt the presence of his mate as a kestrel circled overhead.

"One more time John, the signal, what is it?" Paddy asked for a third time.

"*Two yards to the left*, if everything is okay, *two yards to the right* if there's a trap, that's it, nothing more", John replied.

"That's it sur, ye heve it now John."

Paddy slurped the last of the tea and threw the spent leaves from the cup onto the moss. Steam rose up and joined the cool mist. The three men shook hands and went their separate ways. They waited.

Chapter 19

Tiny Tony flung his hat across his desk and a cup of pens and pencils went flying, tinkling onto the side of the radiator in his grey office.

"Bastards to hell, why me? Why me Jesus? I have done everything you've asked and more, have I not done enough penance in this place? I want to go home, seriously." Tony was as crabbit as ten bags of cats. Tom could hear the commotion and put two and two together that the raid was a farce. He walked as far as the doorway and peered in, with half his body protected by the wide white frame.

"That bad, what?" Tom rubbed his black moustache and spoke gingerly to the back of Tony's head.

"You and your informer, my fucken arse", Tony swung around at his colleague. He had picked up a handful of the scattered pens from the floor and fired them at the door. Tom jumped out of the way. He hoped that Tony would see the funny side later as they had a quiet pint in the Cottage Bar, but for now, he would take a bit of settling as his fat, jouley cheeks reddened with rage and humiliation.

"And another ting", Tony spoke to the empty doorway, knowing that Tom was listening on the other side, "dat old Leo, dat old bloody lunatic by the fingerpost, if I ever see him pissing in a public place again, dat old bugger, one more time, he'll be jailed, so help me, Mother of God". Tony slumped into his chair and the wheels groaned and screeched on the cold timber floor.

Tom entered the room and sat tentatively on the other side of the desk.

"That bad, what?", he asked again.

"Worse than bad. When we found the holy water he laughed at us and offered us a blessing from Knock. I would have laughed only I was so angry. Your man is exposed, if he wasn't already, he's finished now, but there's more to this one than just shining the light on Tadhg Byrne."

"There's been activity over the border, men escorted across by the RUC, we're watching them and they're looking for a few men, but Dinny is top of the list, a shot across the bow, no safe haven in the free state now, what". Tom replied and he bounced out of the chair, as if a light had been switched on in the dark corner of his mind and rats and ghosts were exposed.

"They're on the move Tony, it was just a distraction, there's been men moved into place in the past few days. Ghosts in caravans at Stragill, new men". Tom's mind raced and he grabbed his coat in a hurry. Tony agreed but thought that however they were moving their man, it was probably too late already.

"C'mon Mick, quick as ye can", Tom barely had time to say *what* as Ass's Teeth followed him out to the car with a mouthful of tea and toast. Tom knew about the den in Augaweel but had kept it to himself. It was the best, worst kept secret in Inishowen and Mick had spoken to a few of Paddy's customers after they had sampled his produce, when they were eager to talk with a steaming belly full of bad manners and wobbly wellingtons, about the badness of Paddy and his high prices for nothing more than polluted water. It was tolerated in the grand scheme of things and, for the most part, kept the potato field cash economy ticking. Although the house had been raided many times, they stayed away from the new den, out of sight, out of mind, and the sanctity of the wee still was respected. Unless it was a direction from the highest level, men like Paddy were worth more to them with pound notes in their pockets, because a hungry man was a dangerous man, and a watched man was a careful man. Ghosts on the other hand, well, ghosts could be anyone and the only way to get to know them was through men like Paddy. If Dinny was still in the Parish, and if he wasn't hiding out at Peter Mulligan's, then the den was the next best place. Minutes were precious as they put the blue flashing light on the roof and sped off without the siren.

John lay still at the lookout. He laid out two empty 10/10/20 fertiliser bags on the wet moss and lay face down with his elbows dug firmly into the soft peat. He cut three palm branches from the lower limbs of the nearest tree and pulled them over his back. It was almost comfortable and if everything went off ok, it was an easy day's pay for Betty after the news this evening. When he closed his eyes for more than five seconds, he heard the beating of his own heart, thumping in his chest and pumping in his ears, furiously letting him know that this wasn't a birdwatching gig, and, above everything else, he needed to stay alert. A passing bird would pay no heed to the green clump at the edge of the clearing. John held the two-way at the ready, poised, channel 27, full battery, green light, set. He watched and waited on the Holy Father and visualised his arrival. Audi 100, gunmetal grey, brylcreem-haired, red and glistening olive face, dead eyes, Guinness fattened gut, white shirt, stench of beer and smoke, tired looking. Easy.

I was more than uneasy with the scene. I saw the dangers, sensed the death in the air but couldn't see the Queen anywhere. The fact that Con had visited him was either a warning, a blessing or a premonition of John passing. I lay under the branches with my boy. The pine needles caught the wind and cocooned the world from around him. About fifty metres behind, and to the left of the clearing, a marksman had John's temple firmly within the crosshairs of his sights. I looked for the Queen again, but she was nowhere to be seen.

Chapter 20

Leo's words had the Holy Father spooked. He thought about cancelling everything and waiting another few days, but if Dinny was already compromised, and they had eyes on him, then the best thing was to get him out, no matter what, and quickly. He had planned the escape route out over Mamore Gap where the mountain road had rolling boulders on either side, rising fifty feet into the air in parts. It was one of the most beautiful roads in Donegal, where the climb to the summit from the Parish side revealed the green fields of Urris and the expanse of the Atlantic Ocean beyond. The sides of the road looked like a sneeze from a mountain goat could cause a great avalanche of stones to block the narrow road. It had way too many vantage points for snipers to launch a surprise attack. Poteen makers in the 1700s did exactly that when they knew the guagers and excise men were on a raid and Urris and Parish men were transported to New South Wales and Van Diemen's Land for their crimes. The statue to Mother Mary nestled at the pinnacle might keep travellers safe, but the Holy Father couldn't rely on Mary alone this time.

He was now more likely to drive over Bulbin where there were less vantage points for a sniper in the flat heather and peat banks, but it wasn't a foolproof escape by any means. He blessed himself as he drove to the pickup point at Augaweel and sat with the engine running. His hands were clammy and sweat formed on his forehead. He felt like a sitting duck, and it was quiet, way too quiet.

John pressed the button on the two-way and spoke in a low, monotonous tone: "Two yards to the left."

"Heve ye now", Paddy replied, and he stepped out into the middle of the muddy haul road and waved his arms, criss-crossing them above his head three times. Peter was relieved to see him and drove into the gravel hard stand and turned to face the main road again. He was within three metres of the nearest line of trees. The doors were unlocked. The car revved naturally, and Peter's right foot tapped the pedal in uneasy anticipation. He leaned across and pushed open the back passenger door and his hands returned to the steering wheel, gripping it with white knuckles like Old Jack on a Sunday morning. Dinny had ten, maybe fifteen, steps before launching himself into the back seat. His heart raced inside his well-built frame. His normally well-shaved face that showcased his black moustache, had morphed into a wild man's grizzly beard. A week of Paddy's hospitality in the den meant ample tea and smokes but didn't extend to razors and he was more rugged than refined. He pinned his ears back and made a run for it, taking up the whole back seat, he pulled the door behind him, and Peter spun off, making his way to the bottom of the Parish and the drive over Bulbin to Clonmany. Muck spattered onto the listening device in the wheel arch, but it sent a perfect signal to the observers.

John was still in position at the lookout and the sniper never let him from his sights. His finger rested comfortably on the trigger, like an extension of himself. He was trained for this. There were no emotions, only orders. Combatant's reasons, circumstances, beliefs and prejudices meant nothing to him. He saw the target, he took the shot, his mission successful and he'd sleep well tonight, knowing he did his job. He learned early on that they were never to say sorry, no matter how dire their mission, no matter if they believed what they were doing was right or wrong. That was work for diplomats and politicians to appease the masses and weekly meetings with royalty. He pulled back and made a swift retreat to the exit point. Their mission was successful, they got what they wanted, and they had full knowledge of their target. He hoped for a warmer war on his next posting, a theatre with sunshine, maybe Belize, West Germany, or Gibraltar, anywhere but traipsing through the North. In his mind's eye, the forestry was twenty miles to the east and the green light was given. Normal rules of engagement applied. He was allowed to ply his trade and there were three less Irish troublemakers alive.

Tom and Mick drove out through the Backhill and met the red Capri on a narrow stretch of road near the old national school at Sledrin. Crows nested in the bare sycamore trees. In the overgrown yard, new saplings grew around and between the stone walls. Half the roof was missing, and the fear of the past students leapt out from every broken window. It felt haunted, it was haunted, and, to many locals, it was unlucky land. Betty had gone to school there before being moved down to the Parish school, where the pain inflicted on her by Miss

Chapman, whose uncle was a Monsignor, was still felt in Keelogs. Sledrin was a relic of old decency, and Betty's spirit still stood at the front seat with her friend Kathleen as they sang for the visiting priest. I heard them singing sweetly as both cars came to a halt, bumper to bumper, neither one moving. The man in the back of the Capri slowly reached for his gun. They were on intelligence gathering in a foreign country, but there were no apologies needed, and the two Irish detectives needed to move out of their way quietly, no one would be hurt, and no one would be any the wiser.

The standoff lasted three minutes and the spirits of the children stood on chairs and desks looking out the windows, quietly watching, feeling the tension between the occupants of each car. Tom and the Capri driver indicated to each other to step out and chat. They opened their doors at the same time and Ass's Teeth quietly disengaged the safety catch on his revolver. The two men stood between the cars.

"You're a long way from home, what?" Tom asked as he nodded towards the Augaweel mountains.

"I'm closer to home than you are", Norman Harris replied in a Belfast accent.

"You're on foreign soil now, away home with ye", Tom stood tall and straight against his British counterpart. Norman was a stocky character, well-built and had just enough hair on his head to say he wasn't bald. He wore a black t-shirt and his arms were short, muscley, tattooed, hairless and strong.

"We'll go when we're ready", he replied indignantly, as he claimed his right to drive where he wanted and go where he pleased, anywhere on the island of Ireland.

"You'll go now, and I'll escort you to the border. Whatever your business was here, give yourself an early day, what." Tom spoke down to him in stature and command. He could tell that the man in front of him was used to getting his own way and had runs on the board since his first day on the job. It was more than a job for Norman, it was his way of life, and tracking volunteers was personal.

"We appreciate the influx of sterling into the local economy, but we don't need any more tourists at the moment," Tom added and rubbed his moustache thoughtfully. A wry smile developed across his dark features.

Norman looked back at his counterparts. They looked straight ahead without blinking. He called the shots on this one and the last thing his commanding officers or Mrs Thatcher wanted was a diplomatic incident in the wild hills of Donegal and explaining it at the weekly meeting with Her Majesty.

"You know, this is a lovely part of the world, but you're right, I've seen enough sights for one day", Norman replied. "Too many stones and wet bogland over this side anyway, that's why we gave it away", and the two men smiled openly, from the teeth out, exactly what the saying was invented for.

"Through the border at Coshquin or Muff?" Tom asked.

"Coshquin", he replied.

"I'll stay behind you, to ensure you get home safe, in time for your lunch. There's lovely spots around the Giants Causeway I hear, if you would like to take your English tourists there, it's a great day out altogether, what." Tom put a shot across the bow and another three across the border.

"What's your name?" Tom asked as both men disengaged and walked towards their drivers' doors.

"It's Jack, nice to meet you Tom", Norman almost laughed.

"It's nice to finally meet you, Mr Harris, it's been a long time coming."

Tom smiled back as he indicated for them to reverse at the school wall and head up towards the crossroads and back to Buncrana. The children cheered from the windows; it was the best thing they'd seen since the school closed and the crows moved in. Betty was glad to see them leave, and she looked out through the last remaining small paned glass window, seeing the red car in the crosshairs of the frame, like they had viewed John earlier. She wished them a speedy journey back over the border and she was overjoyed that John was safe.

The potatoes had broken through the soil. Each day they reached further and higher towards the sun. The greatest harvest in history was a mere formality. Perfect amounts of rain, gentle breeze, sun and cloud cover would make this year's crop the best ever. The farmer stood back, feeling proud of the fresh green tops in the field. Gaps in the hedges that she would normally stuff with whun bushes to stop neighbours checking the progress of the potatoes were left off. There was nothing not to like, nothing to hide. She felt great pride, pure Donegal, TirConnell pride. The young man appeared again and walked across the drills. He had his back to her, and she knew him, she called to him, but he carried on, waving the back of his hand in farewell as he walked towards the white mist. She called his name this time. "John, are ye away?" and he was almost out of sight before he stopped and looked back. He smiled and turned back towards her, face beaming with love and his bright green eyes shone under dark heavy brows. The potato tops were undamaged, his steps light, taken in the other world, seen here. His time would come, but not today.

Chapter 21

Paddy drove the Mark III Cortina to the top of Augaweel hill when the Holy Father and Dinny were gone. He stayed in radio contact with John until he got to the gap at the foot of the brae and the coast was clear. He opened the sheep wire gate and peeled it back towards the ditch. Brockie ewes with straggly wool and red paint on their backs stopped grazing the short, pebble dunged, mossy grass and watched him, hoping he left the gate open long enough for them to escape to better feed in the fields below. Their eyes were wild, almost deranged, and they bore the scars of the cold winter they had endured. Cold as the winter was, hard as their existence was, however futile anyone thought their life was, they were more than proud to parade their beautiful lambs behind them in the hope that their children's future was brighter than their own. Paddy acknowledged their stoicism and pride.

Most people in the Parish had a bank of turf out here, handed down from generation to generation. Even though the hill was privately owned, the rights were respected, and the owner could be found in Phil Hegarty's or Flaherty's for the payment of the rent there. The bank was cut from a straight face of black and brown peat, about six feet deep. The turf was cut into four-inch square sections, around a foot long and turned, stood up and dried in the summer months for the winter fires. Paddy hoped that he had the hill to himself today and looked across at the black vertical faces of at least one hundred banks. He hated working turf more than he hated gathering potatoes, lifting corn, drying hay, or any farming that involved a sore back at the end of the day. After today, he would be glad to get back to doing what he did best, making the finest poteen in Ireland.

Paddy drove the car slowly through a low section of the cobbled road, covered with a foot of black, peat-rich water. It parted like a tidal wave of molasses and the rushes scraped under the car and steam rose, as the exhaust gave off muffled petrol fumes and a burnt oil smell. He pulled up and removed the number and compliance plates and buried them. He drove another hundred yards and pulled off to the side, scraping through rushes and heather. The car bogged and spun in the wet moss; it was as good a place as any. He doused the car in petrol and after lighting a calming smoke, flicked the match and set it alight. He watched the flames grow in excitement and intensity. The black smoke rose, and the metallic sounds of expanding steel and tyre wires exploding at will made it feel alive, burning itself at will with a mind of its own, thankful for the fuel and the match. Finally, the petrol tank went up and the car shook like a barricade in Derry. It was a satisfying end to Dinny's holiday in Augaweel and Paddy was glad that the responsibility of his safety and security now lay elsewhere. The flames danced in Paddy's wild eyes, he considered it a bonfire just for himself, and he couldn't help feeling like it was an ancient Druid ritual with a modern twist. The Queen stood beside him and warmed her white hands at the fire. She acknowledged that the danger had passed for now, but they'd be back. The tracking device under the boot lid ceased to be useful and it pinged for the last time in the barren hill in Donegal, but they were two for a penny, and as one stopped, two more took its place.

Barney Breen lay in against his turf bank and sheltered from the wind. His twenty-eight-inch daisybell bicycle lay up near the road, with the steel brake lines well lubricated with three in one oil. He was a bachelor like Old Jack, but it wasn't for want of trying or two old aunts that he was wifeless. He hadn't been blessed from birth with Old Jack's height, looks and charisma and he cursed his short father and odd mother for it. He had a red, fat face, like a pressurised vessel containing hot gas, hard for a man like me to describe, but he resembled something of a cross between an overripe carrot and a black pot belly stove. His eyes were googly, stark and frightening to make direct contact with. His grey hair was straight as a rush and poked out of his tweed cap like a retired scarecrow. Barney had thatch on his roof too, but each stalk of rye was just that, rye, dry, musty sheaves of Irish grass and not a woman of any kind in sight. He had just warmed up enough to take off his old suit jacket when he saw Paddy burning the car. He was fairly sure who it was, and although it was none of his business, everything was Barney's business, and he wasn't called the Inishowen Echo for nothing. He'd keep this in his memory bank for a later date.

-

Tom was animated after his meeting with Norman. They usually viewed each other from a distance, through high powered lenses and monotonous hours of watching, observing and reporting, rarely taking action and never meeting in person. Cross-border relationships were tense at the best of times, but in the next few months there would be a heightened alert, and broad daylight espionage or worse, cross-border abductions, would not be tolerated. Diplomatic relations were strong as far as Dublin, Belfast and London were concerned, but it was a daily challenge on the ground. Tom and Mick pulled into the layby at Bridgend and watched the red Capri leave the Republic and disappear onto the smooth British roads with a knowing wave of a soldier's hand at the Coshquin crossing. They turned around and headed straight for the Augaweel den. Paddy would either answer some hard questions, or he'd be hounded on a daily basis, and every drop of his famous brew would end up in the bellies of Atlantic salmon in Lough Swilly.

The mountain wind carried the black smoke over Barney as he laboured with a broad spade and dug the turf in small, but neat cuts, laying them out in rows, like glistening, perfect scales of a salmon. He cursed the sooty smell of the burning rubber and the sweet smell of burnt oil and petrol. *Them boys never had a titter of wit, sure as Jesus, he's going to hell for burnin' a perfectly good yok*, he said to himself, and it was a sure-fire sign of a madman to walk home from Augaweel after burning his own transport.

Seeing Barney in his element, listening to him muttering to himself, answering himself back and laughing at the response, I was glad that Con only visited on very rare occasions and was already gone. If anything, or anyone, would keep him away from the world as you know it, it was Barney Breen. Con's last three seasons in Augaweel were the wettest summers on record and every time the turf seemed to be hardening, getting a crust and cracking in the sun, the rain started and plashed the hill until the river at the foot of the banks overflowed and the turf went backwards, back to a sodden glug of mass peat again. The rain did stop occasionally. Con seized these days and borrowed his brother's tractor, and with his four sons sitting on the bare mudguards and link box on the back, he drove the four miles out to Augaweel, stopping off at Brigid Mary Whites to fill old cidona bottles and the grey kettle with water from the well. They stuck a potato in the stroop of the kettle before being shook and losing most of its contents on the cobbled and potholed tracks. Con guzzled four fresh cups of spring well water like a delirious madman at an oasis who had crossed the Sahara for three days straight. It eventually softened the sandpaper and dust off his tongue from Flaherty's oasis and top shelf last night. His mood was never great, in fact it was diabolical, and the young fellas held their whist and followed instructions best they could. They worked hard as the sun shone or at least the rolling clouds held their water to themselves, but every time Con saw Barney coming in the cobble road on the daisybell, he cursed him to high Heaven. He appeared as a black speck rising from the heather, like an annoying midge that lay dormant in the undergrowth until disturbed and rose to bite your face until you went mad inside your own skin.

"Fucken weathers broke now boys, Barney's here." Con stopped and cracked open the tobacco tin for the last smoke in the dry. Sure enough, every time, the Heavens opened. They'd work through the rain and hold fertiliser bags over their heads until eventually they drove home saturated, as the rain drove at them harder as they picked up speed on the bare tractor frame. The black smoke from the Super Dexta exhaust was the only semblance of heat between Augaweel and Keelogs. As they drove past Barney, he'd look up and smile, beaming a beetroot radiance at them, and Con, after having lit the rollie six times already, threw the sodden remains of the cigarette in his direction and cried on the inside, pleading with God to allow him back to the sanctity, safety and security of the British tunnels and away from the misery of Donegal farming.

Chapter 22

Paddy made it back to the sheep gap at the bottom of the hill and jumped over the wire rather than opening it again. He looked back towards the peak, and the smoke from the Cortina was no more than what Con Devenney would have made boiling a kettle of tea and hard-boiling eggs when he was here. He caught the attention of the scraggly sheep again and they followed him with interest through their sullen eyes. He thought about trying the jolly swagman trick and cutting one up for the tucker bag. Surely, they'd never miss one. He smiled at the thought, and the ewes made a quick skip backwards and stood in front of their babies like any mother would. Paddy saluted their tenacity, lucky for them, he was a brewer not a butcher and, anyway, if there was one thing that he despised more than people licking the ends of their fingers, it was the smell of fresh lamb chops and greedy men sucking meat from the bones of the small animals. He shivered and ran as far as the main road. He took a shortcut through the fields and was almost at the den when he heard the detective's car, smoothly and quietly making its way to the spot that Dinny was picked up from.

He watched Tom and Mick analyse the tyre tracks and they walked in the rest of the way. Paddy knew that there had to be consequences for using the Altar Boy this morning. Men like Tadhg, trusted men, were hard to come by and it would be seen as a personal affront to the whole Garda station. He sensed another Buncrana Law Day, another good sized fine and he readied himself for the run to Mountjoy with a note on his back telling the chief warden to keep him for a month this time, whether you have room or not, let him sleep in the coal house with the rats or work him in the kitchen peeling perdies and washing dishes. Whatever the outcome, Paddy would take what was coming with a smile; he was never as glad of anything in his life as he was to see the back of Dinny this morning. He watched the Guards leaving, as sullen faced as the brockie ewes on a wild night in Augaweel, and he determined that he'd get in front of them under his own terms in the next day or so, because it was better to be on the front foot and own the story than be caught like a deer in the headlights.

-

Old Jack looked out the small, white, four paned window by the dresser onto Drumfad hill. He pulled back the lace curtain and nudged his black rimmed glasses further up the crook of his long nose for a better look at the figure in the distance. He squinted his left blind eye, holding the palm of his hand over it to stop its interference with the partly blind right one. It was John walking down through the fields and he was just the man that Jack had been looking for. He had woken this morning from a great dream, although when he opened his eyes, the dream was all but lost and he struggled to remember it. Since he put on his socks, the need to clean out the lower room in Drumfad and getting rid of the crows' nest from the chimney was a high priority. It hadn't really bothered him all winter, but it was a springtime job, and he would think shame if the door should unlatch, and the cut of the room would bring the ire of his dead aunts and the realisation that he had let their pride and joy go to wrack and ruin. He watched the black figure disappear behind the ditch. An unmarked Garda car drove slowly down Drumfad Road, and the two burly plainclothes men had their windows down with their arms resting on the sills of the doors, cool as cucumbers, like they were landlords surveying their property, sneering in at the cut of the nettles and overgrown Schoch's behind the thatched house.

Old Jack moved his curtain as the passenger looked in, and their eyes met, as much as anyone could meet Jack's eyes, and Mick thought he was staring at a blind man and surely he didn't still have a licence for the badly parked car with the bonnet pinned against the low wall in the street. It felt like they had interest in Drumfad, like they were suspicious of Jack for not having placed the right amount in Sunday's envelope at Cockhill Chapel. Jack was a young man once too, like all old men were, and he wished that he was twenty-five again to bid the two of them a fair fight with no gloves, after which Drumfad would be a Guard-free zone.

John checked the depth of Old Jack's well through the gap in the flagstones. It was as full as he'd ever seen it. In the last frost, Jack had turned on the tap opposite his front door when the pipes were frozen but forgot to turn it off again. As the pipes thawed and Jack spent two full days in Keelogs, the spring well drained as dry as a cornflake and airlocked to go with it. John did all the maintenance, whether he could do it or not. He jumped out onto the road five minutes after Tom and Mick had passed and Old Jack stood at the gable of the house facing Stragill waving him in.

"Did ye see the Guards there?" Jack asked, with his hands in his trouser pockets in his usual bandy-legged pose.

"Saw there rightly", John replied, not wanting to give away the fact that he'd hidden from them and get Jack going about his days of being in bother.

"Aye, you saw them, I know rightly, but they didn't see you. Are ye in bother?" Old Jack asked, partly as a father figure, partly as a roommate and partly as a news fender.

"No bother Jack. We all look the same, and our Eamon gave them boys a bit of cheek when they lifted him, best to stay out of their road."

John laughed and followed Jack into the house, ducking his head at the doorway for the first time. This made him feel like a man as he remembered not being able to see over the half door when Old Jack was teaching him to read and write and count to one hundred.

"Heve ye time to clear out the lower room chimney and set a fire, for it's wild musty down there?" Jack asked, as he put a thin, Indian meal scone into the oven like a true TirConnell bachelor.

"Man made time, made plenty of it, Jack." John laughed at the stupidity of time and people gurnin' about having none, then wasting their lives crying at the speed of time. He opened the lower room door, and the thin twigs were scattered over the floorboards around the hearth like a wicker woman's workshop. He sensed his father standing beside him and heard him gasp another *"Humph"* and crack up with laughter. They both looked at the ceiling in case Sally Anne was still in her passionate embrace with the love of her life, but the only shadows were the overgrown nettles and hawthorns waving in the window.

Old Jack stood at the doorway and sighed, somehow, in some realm of existence or frequency, he remembered last night. It was the best night of his life, and he was guilt-free. The room had to be tidied at all costs in case she came back tonight for the second-best night of his life.

"The ladder is in the byre and if ye have enough time, can ye take the scythe to the nettles and grass at the back Schoch?" Jack twitched his tongue and his mouth watered at the thought of his Indian meal scone with the tea later. It was nothing like Betty's treacle, carraway or raisin scones, but it filled the gap until his tea at Keelogs and was better than bought bread. John was already on the roof and pushing the remaining twigs down into the hearth below with the end of a yard brush. He heard the echoed and muffled instruction coming up the chimney and carried on. John made a wigwam of Friday's Derry Journal and twigs and struck the match. The smoke rose slowly and sat on the thatch like a white cloud, allowing worlds to meet.

Jack cut the scone towards his body, in slow swards, like a man cutting corn with a scythe. The breadcrumbs dropped on the stone floor and the old man concentrated, best as he could see. The tea plumped, strong, pungent and black on the gas. Jack was glad of the company and having John at the house gave it a youthful feel, like the house had just been built and there was hope for what was coming tomorrow. He knew that John had no fear, and if he didn't love the boy like a son, he'd be envious of his free spirit, but his love of John and all the Devenneys for taking him in was unconditional. He wouldn't spend a night in Drumfad if Cassius Clay was to give him all his millions or he won the lottery. The back Schoch was clear of nettles now, but the fact remained, in daylight or darkness, that the Banshee had visited there on the night of his last aunt's passing. Even now, cutting the scone and listening to the swish of the scythe outside, he could still hear the three knocks at the door as Old Alice was rasping with a foot in both worlds. He answered the door, but there was no one there. He walked around the gable on that calm, still, dark night and there she was, looking in the back window at the candlelit scene. She cried the most mournful cry that TirConnell had ever heard. She turned to face Jack and held her arms in the air and continued. Her small stature and black cloak and scarf branded Jack's mind forever. When he finally ran back inside, Alice was already gone, making her way out over the hill with the Irish messenger from God. He sat with her until the first light of day, frozen and numb, swearing to never spend another night there, no matter how many women adorned the roof.

"Do you think you'll marry, Jack?" John said with a smile as he pulled on the tough, thin scone bread.

"Aye, maybe at the end of the summer when I sell the bullocks at Burnfoot mart." Old Jack loved banter more than anyone and it kept his heart ticking.

"One from the roof Jack? Or how about Molly Murphy up the town street, she has a great word on ye and admires your car with the four doors and fancy steering wheel."

"John, yer a grand young fella, but I wouldn't pish on Molly Murphy if she was on fire", Jack replied and slapped his tweed cap on his knee.

He loved the fact that with John in the house, he couldn't hear the clock ticking and, whether he liked it or not, he couldn't take himself seriously, which was more than fine with him. The banter was the best part of being in Keelogs and he liked to think that he had a hand in making John what he was today. He thought about him twenty years from now, when John would be a man of nearly thirty-five, and he would come to weed the grass from the daisies over his head at Cockhill and say an Ave there. He'd roll over for a second sleep, his feet warm under the blankets and the fire dancing on the ceiling, glad that he knew and loved him since he was a child.

Chapter 23

Bad news travelled fast. Every visitor to a shop, pub or garage had the news. The coal man carried heavy black bags on his back into houses and out into the back yards, sweating, coughing, laughing and recounting the story that he was told, all the while adding a bit on to suit himself. By the time the Altar Boy heard how the raid went, Ted had been arrested for firearms offences and was on his way to Mountjoy, but the fact remained, there wasn't a skerrick of clear liquid at his place except the holy water from Knock. There must have been some mistake. They mustn't have looked right. Tadhg had bet his future career on this, and he could imagine the heads on Tom and Mick, Tom what, what whatin' and rubbing his black moustache. He reasoned with himself that one bad piece of intel was acceptable and even the best of undercover men get it wrong sometimes. He knew that Tony was on the raid, and he hated being wrong more than being called Tiny. If everything was lost for this, then he'd be taking the law into his own hands and wiping the smile from a wheen of faces, starting with John Devenney and Paddy Ennis. He didn't exactly know how yet, but they were up to their necks in it. He'd have to face the music in the meantime and went out to the General's shop phone box to call Tom for a meeting.

Liam met John at the foot of Drumfad Road. He had walked out with Andy and held him up by the two front paws. Andy was afraid of nothing when he was walking on two paws and very little on four, the same as John. When he walked with Liam, it was mostly on his two back legs and he never growled at the boy, being as thankful as Old Jack to be in Keelogs with a warm bed, pleasant company and scone bread. It was a small price to pay and although it seemed random for a dog to be dumped and end up here, like everything else, it was anything but random: he had been sent by Con to look after Liam.

"Are ye ready for the news, John?" Liam walked alongside his brother with the dog.

"No news tonight, Liam, the electricity has been cut to the TV", John replied and walked in the back gate, smiling, waiting on the response.

"It's not even hooked up sur", Liam replied and laughed, throwing a stone for Andy to catch as he sat on the chair outside the car shed.

John gave his mother a hug and looked down on the top of her head for the first time. Maybe she was shrinking, he thought. John was taking his place amongst men, as the boy in Glasgow seemed to have stalled in his growth and the t-shirts, jeans and shoes were all too tight in Josie's parcel. He had grown in size over the past six months and grown as a man in the past two weeks. Soon, he thought, he'd be in London, San Francisco or Sydney, where time wasn't just time, but hour by hour, day by day, time was money, and he'd light the fire with ten-dollar notes like Muhammad Ali and George Foreman after their rumble in the jungle.

Betty remembered the promise he had made to never leave Keelogs and always stay close to her, as she cried in despair when the older boys left for London and beyond. Without holding them back, she reasoned there must be enough work at home to stop them going to other countries. It was hopeless, the whole emigration thing, the notion that they couldn't be born, live, work, marry, grow old and die in their own country. John hugged his mother that day as the thought of losing his older brothers was like entering an empty wake house: no one came with condolences, tins of biscuits, scones or extra chairs for the mourners. The next day, with the packed bag from inside the front door gone, there was an emptiness, a cold loneliness in Keelogs that lasted for weeks, as TirConnell and anyone worth asking knew they would never live in Ireland again.

John went out to the car shed for the news and Betty sat on the chair next to Liam.

"Good evening and welcome to the Keelogs RTE 1 news at ten past six. It's Wednesday 18th March 1981. Making news this evening, Paddy Ennis has gone to Manchester for a holiday and drove his Escort van over on the ferry to Liverpool. When he got there, he drove through green, orange and red lights at full pelt. He drove the same way that he drove at home, by intention and familiarity, with most people knowing where he was going anyway. There was no need for indicators or brake lights when he knew the road and the road knew him. When the police stopped him, he rolled down the window to see what was wrong.

"The policeman said 'Sir, do you know you've driven through four sets of red lights, two stop signs and two give way signs and almost caused multiple accidents?'

"'Lights, signs, what signs?' Paddy replied. 'Niver seen them sur, the way I drive, y'see sur, if ye can go, ye go and if ye can pass, ye pass. Simple drivin', safe drivin', effective, ye know what I mean sur?' Paddy smiled and looked up at the constable with the black notepad in his hand.

"'Get out of my sight Paddy and carry on, and the next time you come to a red light you STOP, understood?'

"Aye." Paddy replied.

"As Paddy drove off, he threw his head back in laughter. He turned to his passenger and asked, 'How the fuck did he know my name?'

"In other news, there has been vandalism to the political posters nailed to the telegraph poles on the way to the Parish post office. Any man caught doing this sort of carry on will be dealt with by the Guards."

"What do ye mean, John, posters?" Liam asked and John didn't hear.

"Councillor Eddie Fullerton's face has been superimposed on the Fine Gael and Fianna Fail candidates' faces. The culprits were last seen carrying a red timber ladder and placing it on the roof in Keelogs. RTE 1 has reported that the old posters look the better for it and Eddie's face is to remain there until after the election."

"You put it there, I saw ye", Liam spoke to the TV and made a bee line for the crash tackle. There was no time for the UTV news. The signal was lost. The wrack was on.

-

"You're finished, I'm sorry Tadhg, we can't use your information from here on, orders from above, what." Tom was half sorry for cutting him loose and half mad at the affront and fallout from the station. There was no doubt in his mind that his Northern neighbours were at least two steps ahead of him, just how far ahead remained to be seen if Dinny turned up or he cornered Paddy.

"What about all the good information I gave youse boys over the years, is it all gone because of one mistake?" The Altar Boy was mad as hell, and he wasn't going away without a fight.

"It might be better if you moved to another town", Mick added, "somewhere like Letterkenny or as far as Killybegs, where no one knows you, maybe get a job on a trawler and start again."

As the thought left Mick's brain and the words left his mouth, he realised there was nothing out there for the Altar Boy. Being an informer was the only thing he was good at. He imagined the ten-foot waves in the Atlantic and the trawler smashing down the side of another white mountain of water and Tadgh, wet, frozen weak and foundered, trying to clear a net with his soft, white hands, shrivelled to prunes, bent, sore and useless. He'd last a day on the high seas and the fish would eat him for breakfast as the crew threw him overboard. No, if there wasn't a job in Ballbofey selling men's shirts and pyjamas in a warm shop with plush carpet and central heating, then the future looked bleak for their ex-friend.

Tadhg looked at them in a vile, wretched, but condescending way, as if he'd just stepped in a huge pile of horse dung, as if he was above them in the pecking order. He turned his back and walked away from the detectives on the shore front of Buncrana for the last time. He had scores to settle before going anywhere and he thought about his poor mother and her only child having to move out of the house. Even though he was only small fry in the scheme of things, the lowest man on the rung was generally the easiest to take out, and John Devenney wasn't going to know what hit him when the Altar Boy went through the fight scene again from the other night. He landed a few solid shots on John and opened the cut above his eye again, that had to count for something. Yes, he'd try again, and if he got the right information, then all this poteen story would blow over. A week was a long time in the intelligence world. I sensed his rage, and his retribution would be over my dead body, literally.

Chapter 24

The postman drove a small green van and had a shop in the main street of Buncrana where he sold newspapers, cigarettes and sweets. He knew everyone there was to know and was very happy with his job, being dry, warm, clean and paid every week of the year. He was so happy that he waved to everyone on the road, regardless of their registration plates being from Antrim, Armagh, Carlow, Cavan, Clare, Cork, Derry or Donegal, or whether they'd wave back or not. He knew all the cross dogs on his run and their barking owners and could tell if your mail was looking for money or had money in it.

He drove up the lane at Keelogs and reversed by the front door. The airmail letter for Betty was a good one and it carried itself differently to the others in the pile. There was a padding, an insulation that only came from worn green backs inside that had already been handed over thousands of times, in countless transactions, somewhere in the great land of America. He stuck his arm out the window with the blue and red stripe edged envelope and was glad to see help arriving where it was needed. They spoke briefly about the weather on the step and what the showers were doing in the forenoon and what they would be doing in the afternoon, before he took off for the whole Parish run.

Betty walked into the kitchen and Andy followed her, wagging his brushy tail, as if he knew it was a letter from one of the boys. The clock began to tick louder as the earlier wind became calm and still. She pressed around the edges of the envelope and marvelled that her own son would think on her from so far away. As always, the sacred heart of Jesus looked down from the gable wall in the kitchen and his face suited every mood, every situation, and with his outstretched nail damaged hands, he was impressed that, like himself, the boys from Keelogs loved their mother. She sat the envelope on the table and looked past it out the window, past the car shed, past the ash tree and past the white pillars, to the glistening Lough below. The clouds parted and the sun shone the brightest it had since before Christmas. The letter sparked a memory in the deep inner caverns of her soul, and with Jesus there, they went on a journey, back to see a three-year-old and give her comfort. I stood there beside her as a privileged guide and was allowed to travel back there too and send love. It was one of the only times I was allowed to deviate from John directly and I recall it the best I can now.

It was nighttime in the dead of winter. Long dark nights in Donegal, when the sun seemed to disappear at four o'clock without ever having really shone any light or warmth on the day. Betty held on tight to the dolly that her mother gave her as the only faint warmth in the dormitory came from the yellow light of the window above the doorway. Muffled voices could be heard in the hallway, making no sense, rushed and whispering, impersonal, practical, strangers, dressed the same and their clothes were hard pressed, neat, clean and cold. In her dreams, she was comforted by her mother, and she closed her eyes tightly, trying to drift away into that dimension and be held in her warm, loving arms. We met her there and Betty sat on the side of the bed with herself as a child. Tears of joy and sadness in equal measures streamed down her face, and she cradled the toddler close to her heart. She remembered this, deep within herself and it was the visit from the beautiful stranger that had carried her through. Betty stroked the child's curly hair, and she looked up, quietly, calmly, content and trusting, with her bright blue eyes radiating love. Their bond was like two pieces of a jigsaw puzzle fitting together, almost fifty years apart.

Ghosts of the many babies and infants, buried at the foot of the garden felt the love and came in to see where all the light was coming from. They too sat around the beautiful stranger with the open heart, and the compassion and love eased their spirits, and they were free of this place, finally. The orphanage had been a workhouse for the poor and destitute of Donegal during the famine and the echoes of every lost soul walking the corridors could feel the warmth and love. A boy had been in the garden for a very short time, so short a time that the grass hadn't yet covered the clay with the green lush emerald tones that would make the world forget that he had ever existed. He was familiar to me, and had green eyes and dark, heavy brows, and he sat next to the bed and smiled. He basked in the light and wished that when he came back, he would have a mother like Betty. This was a place of dreams and miracles happened when it was held as true by more than one. Betty embraced the boy as she had embraced her younger self. All the fear and pain was lifted and an eternal bond was created. Myself, Jesus and Betty watched the boy disappear into the light, having waited for this moment before leaving. He would be a brave soul to come back to Donegal after his short and painful life, but brave souls rarely opted for easy lives, and his next one, although seen by many as imperfect, laborious and challenging, would be his best life ever and the world would come to know more love than it ever had because of it. As the light engulfed him, he sent love to his mother in this lifetime, and she grieved the child that she had lost twice in the space of two months, once to the home and finally to God. Their bond was strong and their love powerful, so powerful that they'd meet again, as brothers, as John and Liam, and they would know and love each other in a full life.

Mothers too, some mere children themselves, carrying the shame of fallen virtues and the wrath of the world, joined us that night. I learnt more about love in those dark earth hours than I had in the entire life I had just lived. I could see then why I was allowed to be there, and I was grateful for the opportunity. Hard, solid blockages around my heart dissolved as the dawn broke and, although already on the other side, I felt lighter than I ever had. The child slept the most content and sound sleep since her mother died. The morning was cold outside, and the mist lay white and frosty at the foot of the garden. Tree branches held on to the last of the cold dew and spider webs could be seen, in all their intricacies, dangling between blackthorn branches. Inside the dormitory, it was neither warm nor cold, but grey and empty. Fourteen children were wakened as one, some crying, some laying silently, all pining for their mothers. The mothers were either dead or at the opposite side of the building, pining for their children. All three of us were still there, walking among them. Some held out their hands in friendship and looked beyond the veil. Their faces were gaunt, and they wore the drudgery of winter and the weight of original sin like a cloak of despair on their tiny shoulders, whether they were baptised or not.

Little Betty woke from the greatest sleep. Nuns darted around without making noise, as if a vow of silence had transpired to go with the other ones. She watched them, moving her eyes only, and left her head firmly planted on the pillow to be out of sight and out of mind. They brushed past as if she were invisible, and she wished she was. She felt the draught on her face from their wide habits and smelt the unmistakable smell of incense and Mass. She remembered the soft summer wind blowing up from Stragill as she played with her sister under the ash tree at Keelogs. It was there, and there only, that her mother's face shone brightest, and she called them both onto her knees and sang songs to them. For the first time in her life, she could hear herself breathing, evenly, in and out. Her ears were filled with her own rhythmic sound and although it felt automatic, she had seen what happened when the sounds stopped, and the child in the next bed lay quietly, still and grey, with their eyes open and staring, only to see them lift up and away and their remains to fill the foot of the garden. She smiled, remembering the beautiful stranger last night and, in that instant, she drifted back to Keelogs, and the excitement of another baby coming into the house. She could still hear her mother's voice, but her face was becoming less clear with every passing day, like she had been cast out on a boat and with every gentle wave, she drifted further towards the horizon, until just a dot at the edge of the world. And then...

Chapter 25

"There's going to be another baby for you and Mairead to look after," Sarah Anne held her two daughters on the high bed in the upper room, one on either side. They cradled their mother and carefully played either side of the bump. Mairead was almost four, and ready for school at the end of the summer. She would have new boots to wear, and her daddy would shake her hand, wishing her good luck to wear them and many miles of safe travel to and from Sledrin school. Betty was two years old and wouldn't be the youngest for much longer. She looked forward to the baby coming and with the excitement of her aunts coming to the house in the last few weeks, it felt like Christmas day, every day, and the birth of a child to go with it.

The girls spent a night with their aunt in the Backhill, and the next day, came home to the excitement of a baby sister. Their father held their hands as they greeted baby Alice. Their mother was on strict bed rest and the turf fire was kept going from morning until night. They left her to rest and went with their father, Jack, and Godparents to Cockhill Chapel for the christening. Alice cried softly as the water was poured on her head and Mairead and Betty got to sit on the front seat, looking around at the otherwise empty Chapel, wearing their best Sunday clothes. Swinging their legs in unison as they sat there, it was the best and happiest day of their lives so far. Jack hoisted them onto the back of the pony and trap and their father tucked warm blankets around them. The noise of the horses' hooves on the roadway made them both fall into a dreamy, deep and comfortable sleep.

Three days passed and their mother contracted a fever. The nurse came out from Buncrana on the fifth day and, finally, the doctor was called. The news was bad, and the doctor walked down to the kitchen and spoke to their father under the gaze of the solemn Sacred Heart. He gave him the news that was to change all of their lives. There was no hope. Sepsis had set in and making her more comfortable was all he could offer. The house filled and Sarah Anne's sisters attended her every need and they got Keelogs prepared for a wake as one life entered and one life left. On her last night, she gave the baby to her two spinster sisters. They had a good house, well thatched and neat, halfway to the town and they had money and never would be married as no man was good enough, not even Jack with his fine suit, full head of hair, beautiful eyes, slender body, brown shoes and great style of boxing. They were both devout seamstresses and would never be thatch on his roof or any other man's roof, and that suited them just fine.

A week later, the house had emptied of neighbours. There was a stunned silence in the house. When the clocks scurried behind the range as the light pierced the darkness, they scurried silently and hearts that had been full of hope two weeks ago, were now broken. The baby was gone, and although their father wanted her back, a promise was a promise, and the seamstresses kept their end of the bargain. He had to go back to work. There was no choice. The family would be split and weans had to be fed and looked about. Decisions were made and none were easy. Mairead was old enough and could be looked after by neighbours and stay in Keelogs at night, but Betty could live with her aunt in the Backhill for a while, just until things got sorted. Weeks turned to months and the short days turned to short nights and long days, where the sun never really left the sky and the cuckoo called late into the evening, willing the light to come back as Donegal almost touched the sun. It was on the eve of the summer solstice in 1932, as the Druid Queen prepared for the most important night of the year, that the girl's father broke down. Despite the challenges in front of him, his rational mind took leave of him and headed for the hills. He heard voices and they followed him wherever he went. Since Sarah Anne's death, he asked himself a million times *what if, I should have got the doctor sooner, one day could have made all the difference, it's all my fault.* The voices followed him as he closed his eyes. They chased him while he dreamt and started again as soon as his eyes opened. His mind split in two. He felt unworthy of love as he couldn't love himself. Any chance of being reunited now was gone. The aunt in the Backhill spoke to the priest and it was decided to send Betty to the home, although it mainly housed unmarried mothers, one more child in the dormitory would be neither here nor there and she would be well looked about and fed and watered. The offer was accepted, and times were tough. It was decided that the fewer visits she had, the sooner she would settle, and she'd forget Keelogs, Mairead, the baby and her mother. It made sense in a worldly, earthly view. It was fate. Pure and simple. It was Betty's fate.

Three years passed, and Betty had as many visits from the outside world. After the first six months, she learnt to forget about Keelogs and the old life that she knew. Maybe the world outside ceased to exist, and the new world was now run by the nuns. She took on an independence, an ability to make the most of things and placed an outer, hard-shelled layer around her heart to strengthen her resilience and never allow it to be broken again. A friend in here was more than a friend. Friends were family when it was the only family on offer, and she grew up quickly. She enjoyed the company of the other children and particularly Josie. Their beds were next to each other, and they swapped dolls, night about. Josie's mother lived on the other side of the building and saw her for an hour a day. As the waves had now taken the boat over the edge of the world, Betty's mother was gone completely. Even the dot had disappeared and although she tried to keep the image fresh in her mind, the singing under the ash tree with Mairead was now nothing more than a distant hum and the characters were hazy, dull and quiet. Josie's mother was young, kind and caring and Betty now called her mammy too, even though Josie wasn't sure at the start, there was more than enough love for them both and they ran to her when the one-hour visit started, like two wee orphans.

-

"Straight lines children, straight lines", was the command from way in front, so far in front that the nun giving the instruction was already out of sight and taking her seat in the pew. They went to the same seats every Sunday, and although not clearly marked, it was the section for the children of the unmarried mothers, or some would call them the orphans, but everyone saw them as different, stained, charity cases, self-inflicted charity cases. Some particularly young mothers, felt a black pity on them and thinking on the coins sent in with their own children to school on a Friday for the jam jar for the black babies of Africa, without a bite of rice to eat, these Donegal orphans were somehow lower down the social rung. It seemed easier to give to strangers whose only crime was being born into drought and poverty, rather than poverty, lust and wrongdoing. Betty felt their stares and sometimes looked across at children her own age, sitting proudly between a set of devout parents, paying attention to the priest. They mostly looked away or had their heads turned back towards the front. A boy named Eddie smiled across and picked his nose at the same time, multi-tasking. He broke the gaze as he inspected the findings from his dig and thought about his mother's threats when he played up: *One more word out of ye and ye'll be sittin' with them orphans next Sunday, and ye can go home with them, and the crowd a nuns are welcome te ye.*

He straightened himself up, and from what he could work out based on the wild time that Jesus endured, being scourged, ridiculed and crucified for his troubles, and the suffering of the souls in purgatory, wherever that was, he was glad that he escaped the wrath of the judgemental God and lived in a normal house.

Betty and Josie waited on their mother to arrive from the laundry. She was late. Their mammy was never late. Finally, the door opened, and it screeched with an echo, like the door between the vestry and the Chapel, with the metal door closer dragging on the leading edge, a kind of entrance cymbal where the priest, entered with two Altar boys either side of him in their red and white robes. The movements were heavy. The steps taken were long strides. The man in the suit with his overcoat draped on his arm, just couldn't be. It was father. She hesitated. There was a level of mistrust now and things had changed. She would have been happy to see him turn on his heels and head back to his life, back to Keelogs and the cold fireplace and empty beds and green moss on the whitewashed walls outside the front door. Happiness was where her heart resided, and she had everything she needed here. Father stood beside Betty like a black tower and his eyes radiated from his face like dull lamps on a lighthouse, opening, shutting, opening, watery, windswept, nervous and afraid of his daughter's reaction.

"Do you know why I'm here Betty?" he asked meekly and got down on his knees to be eye to eye with his daughter but, also to beg her forgiveness and undo the wild mistake that had occurred to leave her for more than three minutes, never mind three years.

"Are you here to visit?" she asked, sounding like a child but her question was beyond her years, and she nodded towards the window, in that he should be leaving soon to get back to Keelogs, it was getting dark.

"No, I'm here to take you home Betty, back to Keelogs and Mairead. I have news — I have a new mammy for you and she's very nice." Betty was silent. Her heart sank and she thought about hers and Josie's mammy from the laundry, the warmth of her hugs, her smell, always fresh, always beautiful, and Josie, her forever sister that never asked about her old mammy but willingly shared hers.

"I have a mammy that I share with Josie, can I stay with her, please, I want to stay here." Betty began to cry in the confusion and a young nun with a kind face walked out of the room with Josie. She dropped the doll. Another nun picked it up and placed it on the top of Betty's bag. It was the last time they would see each other for twenty years. Betty was going home to Keelogs where a new mammy was waiting. She hoped upon hope that somehow, miraculously, the new mammy was Josie's mammy, and she could come with them, maybe that was why she was late, already in Keelogs and had good fires on in the upper and lower room and the kitchen warm and smelling of tea and fresh treacle and raisin scone bread. She hoped that they were getting Josie's bag packed and putting on her warm coat for the journey.

Her father stood up again, in his tall, dark stance they were as far away from each other as ever. He held out his hand and she took it, all the time waiting for Josie and her mother to join them. There were muffled conversations that sailed over her head on the way to the front door. All along, she waited on her sister, but the cold corridor was just that, cold and empty. This was a day she would never forget, but it was a day that she tried to never remember.

-

James O'Brien was a proud Chicago policeman. His father too, Irish-born in Galway, wore the uniform shortly after arriving in the city and although the job was dangerous and guns were always loaded, he loved the job, almost as much as he loved his mother. She was one of seven children born down in Cissy McGoldrick's thatched house and was father's aunt. They all moved to Glasgow during the famine and from there, his mother, Mary Anne, immigrated to America and their story began. Small amounts saved over many months, made a big difference and the O'Briens gathered what they could afford and sent it to Keelogs. It was the least they could do to help and in some small way, they felt guilty for leaving the place, but without men like father flying the flag, Ireland would surely sink.

Father arrived home with Betty. She had no recollection of the place as she glanced up the lane at the whitewashed walls, the tin roofs to the outhouses and the blue front door. The ash tree had grown in the past three years and the branches almost overhung the slate roof, shading the kitchen window in summertime. Mairead appeared in the doorway and ran down with open arms and engulfed her sister. Betty was nervous and wanted to go back home to what she knew, to order and friends. Hens pecked around the front step and walked slowly out of the way, like old pet dogs that had become blinded by age. Father lifted Betty when they reached the front door and carried her into the kitchen to meet her new mammy. Her name was Margaret and she was the most beautiful lady that Betty had ever seen. She felt the love of Josie and her mammy beside her as she shook hands with Margaret, and they urged her to go on, to let love in and don't stand back. If three years in the home had taught her anything, it was to reach out to love when it was shown to you, and although her mind wouldn't let her go there, she had seen the flames of love almost extinguished with other children lost in the system. The smell of black plumping tea on the range and a raisin and treacle scone from the oven brought back memories and although they'd hoped that Betty would forget the last three years eventually, it would shape her life and the lives of her children for the next ninety.

Betty stood at the kitchen table and held her doll like a security blanket. Her nose was level with the top of the table and she followed the designs of the tablecloth, daydreaming, taking her mind out of the kitchen for a while and away from being the centre of attention. There was an envelope leant against the sugar bowl. The writing was joined and made no sense, but the colours she knew, they were red and blue and red again around the edges. It looked important, almost lifechanging. The money from the O'Brien clan was Heaven sent. Betty looked past the envelope, out past the window, past the car shed, past the ash tree, past the white pillars and onto the glistening lough below. She soared down there as father whispered to Margaret that the wean needed time to adjust, to get into life on a farm again, and, most of all, for her to trust and love them again. Although the shell would remain around her heart for a lifetime, she would never forget the love in the home, from Josie and her beautiful middle mother, the mother she would never meet again, the mother she would always love and was duty bound to forget.

At the foot of Phonsies' field, still in the townland of Keelogs on the way to the Parish, frogs croaked at the edge of the clearing, and they laid hope in the orangey muck and still water of the schochs by the main road, full of fresh, clean, jellied spawn. They felt the contentedness of the evening and Keelogs felt whole again. The cuckoo sat at the wallsteads on the way to Stragill and sang of a lost love from long ago. The boy at the foot of the garden in the home, felt the same calmness and made plans to call Keelogs home one day and picked out the name John for himself in anticipation. Circumstances, good, bad and indifferent, had set the scene, with many people's input shading the colours and tones of the backdrop. He waited in peace until his call and looked forward to his next life.

Chapter 26

The Altar Boy drove around the town in his Avenger, like he was on a mission to save the world. He met a Garda patrol car at the market square as the traffic stopped for Johnny McGlinchey to drop his wife off to do the shopping in Bradley's. Tadhg nodded to the two Guards, and they ignored him. Maybe they didn't see his gesture as one of their own. He casually wound the window down and gave them a proper Donegal salute with an open-handed wide wave. They ignored him once more. Finally, he gestured for the driver to wind down his window and he stretched his short body and long nose out the window to speak. Mrs McGlinchey slammed the car door and Johnny moved off quickly, seeing the patrol car behind him and the cut of his car, with broken lights, cracked windscreen and enough cow dung and muck on the number plates to start a fertiliser business. The Altar Boy was now holding up six cars behind him and the Guard, a young, tall, green Guard from Sligo knocked loudly on his driver's window.

"Get on wit ya", he shouted through the glass at Tadhg, like he was speaking down to a learner driver, or the town eegit, or both at the same time. The Altar Boy felt the stares of the whole street on the back of his head, and he imagined the loud laughter in McConnell's souvenir shop as weans ordered an ice cream cone and enjoyed the craic, pointing to his fall from grace. The pain was unbearable. There was no time like the present and he headed for Keelogs to sort it out one way or another. He had learnt early in the piece that it was better to fight a proxy war than risk full engagement with a dangerous enemy. The way to Paddy Poteen, the Holy Father and even Tom and Mick, was through young John.

Old Jack had been to the town earlier but got distracted as he was getting into the car and left the pint of milk on the roof. He didn't hear the glass smash on the roadway at the first pothole and cursed when he arrived back in Drumfad until the air turned blue. He did a six-point turn and headed back for another bottle. He was parched, ready for tea and determined to make this a quick run. He met the Altar Boy on the Keelogs brae. He marvelled that even with his limited and sometimes non-existent sight, the sure-fire Garda car opposite him seemed to be driven by the invisible man, either that, or a wean stole it and was taking it for a run through the Parish. The Altar Boy stared out at the old man, knowing that he lived with John Devenney, and was roommates of sorts, lodger, friend, father figure. He'd run the old man off the road, which wouldn't be hard, if he could get away without damaging his own.

-

It was John's 15th birthday today, although a few years ago there was a mix up on exactly how old he was; Betty had to count back on her fingers and count forward from how old Liam was. I wished him many happy returns as my grandson and my godson. He had already turned more corners in his short life than most did in their whole lives. To the best of my ability, I let him know that the Altar Boy was on his way, and he was unpredictable at best and a downright wee lunatic at worst.

-

Paddy Poteen decided to clear out the den. There was absolutely no point in sitting there and waiting to be raided. He walked across to the Backhill, picked up his van and called down to Keelogs to pick up John. He didn't worry about being followed, and the only sinister apparatus was the still itself, every gas bottle and other accoutrement could be explained away. They hid the still and loaded the van to the hilt, removing any evidence that poteen was ever made here. Paddy had had a good run and the poteen might taste different in another place with another water source, but his loyal customers would be none the wiser if it came from a tank, Schoch, a spring or a river, so long as the alcohol content wasn't compromised and the cost was the same. It was time to start brewing in Sledrin Glen anyway, with the added protection of the angriest collie dogs in Donegal at the foot of Rosie Lynch's Lane, they would make any Guard think twice before a raid.

-

Leo stood at the finger post. Three farmers had used the phone today to call for the AI man and the refund chute was paying out fifty pence pieces like show bags at the Parish Bazaar. He bought twenty Carrolls and a fresh box of matches at the post office and lit up, watching the time drift by, one second at a time. The Altar Boy drove past slowly, and Leo observed him with the eyes in the back of his head. To a stranger, he had passed through without being noticed but perceptions in the Parish were deceiving and Leo knew that he was out here fishing, watching and waiting. Fifteen minutes later, Leo saw the car driving back towards Buncrana, having taken the top road. It was worth a call to the Holy Father, and he jingled the loose change in his pocket to dial.

Any man that was parched in the Parish today was out of luck. The Holy Father's smoke signals were non-existent. He was having a day off and was glad of the peace and quiet until the call from Leo. There was always going to be some pushback after the last few days and the Altar Boy was either very brave or very stupid to still be driving in the Parish without an armed escort. His next corner could be his last with a tractor parked broad sides beyond a sharp bend and no reversing. In his mind's eye, Peter saw the scrawny black little figurine dying the death of a thousand screams as he was tied to the pier at the fort until the tide rose above his head, begging for forgiveness rather than moving to Killybegs and anonymity.

The Altar Boy threw caution to the wind. In his rage, all sense of any kind went out the window and his normal surveillance technique of seeing and not being seen was the Tadhg Byrne of the past. He turned up Drumfad Road and peered in at the Keelogs scene. Thick, white smoke chuffed from the drum in the garden, and he screwed up his window as a mixture of plastic, paper, cardboard and potato skins filled the inside of his car. He wondered how people lived like this in the countryside, miles from anywhere and living like uneducated heathens. The wind fanned the flames in the barrel, and he drove on, choking back a fake cough in the back of his tonsils. Betty looked out through the back scullery window. Grass grew on the tin roof above her head, a relic of when Con fixed the leak by putting sods on the roof, to grow a waterproof lawn. She could sense the Altar Boy was trouble, coming from trouble and looking for more. Her mother's instinct told her he was looking for John and she looked up at the sacred heart for guidance and protection.

Paddy and John had set up the new den in the Slederin Glen and would move the still under the cover of darkness tonight. Just being out on the road made the Altar Boy feel like he was doing something constructive and better than packing his bag for the open seas and a life of herring and salt air. He turned down towards the Backhill and would look in at Paddy Poteen from the road. No harm in that, no harm at all. An innocent drive in the fresh air was the right of any Irish citizen, whether they pay their taxes or not. There was a sharp bend next to the entrance of the poteen house. Paddy drove his van the normal way with John as his passenger, flat out and by intention and launched out onto the road like no one else used it. The Altar Boy had been gazing in past the line of pine trees and his hand on the steering wheel watched the road. The smoke was rising from the chimney, but apart from that, the place looked deserted, rough, bachelor rough, but deserted. He didn't have time to look at the road again as the almighty bang and crumpling of metal shook the car. The door pressed in against his left leg in slow motion and his head banged sharply against the steel mullion between the doors. For a time, he was completely knocked out and a red, raised bump developed on his forehead.

It was the first time that John had seen Paddy panic. He had been in plenty of crashes before, not least the one with Dinny that nearly killed him. Plenty of minor batters, bridge walls, pedestrian crossing rails and corners of buildings that jumped out in front of Old Jack's bumper bar, but this one had something that couldn't be fixed, the yapping of the Altar Boy and the charges laid when his friends at the station got out their black booking books.

"Hi sur, yer man come from nowhere sur", Paddy reversed in the lane as bits of glass pulled away and dropped on the road. He ran back out on the road as John was trying to open the passenger door to get the Altar Boy out. He imagined the first thing that the little informer saw was the man he was looking for, rescuing him in a way, and, in his eyes, the man that just tried to kill him. Paddy reached in the driver's door and steered the car down the lane as Tadhg slept like a baby.

"Git this yok aff the road and git him in the house, until a man can think."

Paddy looked in at his nemesis and with John pushing on the boot for all his worth, he laughed a humph laugh, like our Con would do. He pulled up the handbrake when they were close to the front door and channelled him, *a couldn't give a fiddlers fuck*, he thought and laughed at the thought of his court day, on getting three weeks or three months in Mountjoy and could almost taste the custard as the Altar Boy roused himself. Paddy and John dragged him out and sat him on a chair outside the front door. Paddy fanned last Friday's Journal at his face as Tadhg began to speak, making no sense and groggy, like a man having spent his last fiver on a bottle of poteen and then drank himself silly. He cried with anguish and frustration, not knowing if this had been an accident or deliberate or a mixture of both. All he did know was that he hadn't looked at the road for a good ten seconds before the bang.

Chapter 27

All things led to the Backhill and the Holy Father had a fair idea where the Altar Boy was heading. He'd had dealings with Tadhg before and, although he couldn't be trusted, he was useful in so many ways and could keep a back line of communication going with the Buncrana station without a phone call being made. He drove onto Paddy Poteen's street and was greeted by the van, its nose poking out from behind the gable wall. It had a crumpled bonnet, smashed lights, bumper on the ground, number plate on the dash and oil and water on the gravel. The side of the Altar Boy's car had taken a good hit and he could be badly hurt, or worse, dead. If the Guards in Dublin could see their prize yok now. He drove in cautiously and although he knew Paddy wasn't a man for violence, the thought of seeing the Altar Boy laid out with a blanket over him, dead as a door nail, had crossed his mind.

The Altar Boy woke fully to the sound of the Holy Father's car stopping next to him and the man himself stood looking down, rubbing the bristles of his chin in disbelief. He felt like calling for his mother, as if it was going to be his last act on earth and he might disappear without a trace. The thought of mammy out calling through Marian Park that his dinner was ready and waiting on her companion to watch Coronation Street with her, made him cry on the inside. Peter got down on one knee until his eyes were level with Tadhg's and he hesitated before speaking, thinking, pointing in the air, a conversation going on behind his eyes, as if he didn't know exactly what to do with him.

"Mother of good, sweet holy God, what are we going to do with you Tadhg, what indeed?" he said wearily.

"If I have ever offended you, Holy Father, then I'm sorry", Tadhg answered, knowing his life depended on it and his voice cracking with nerves.

"It's Peter to you. Do you believe in God?" he asked, as if he might be sending him to meet his maker.

"I go to Mass", Tadhg replied, trembling, quivering at the thought of his impending death.

"That's not what I asked you, Tadhg. Do you believe in God? If you were to leave here today, this very minute with a shot to the head, would you be in paradise tonight?"

"I can't say as I do then Peter, and you'll never get away with this, I have friends you know."

"The only friend you have is yourself Tadhg, and get away with what? I haven't laid a finger on you. You, me, everybody, we will all die alone and make our own way home, no one can take that journey with you."

Tadhg glanced pleadingly at John sitting on the step and Paddy walking around the street in circles, kicking stones, mad about the van being out of action and this eegit on the street and so much poteen to make and customers waiting. Peter knew that if the Altar Boy was to get back to the barracks in this state, then men would be lifted, including himself, with charges laid, driving with intent. Dangerous driving for Paddy and being an accessory for John would have both of them doing time, not to mention hiding Dinny. He walked over and whispered to Paddy in the middle of the street, glancing back at the Altar Boy every ten seconds. It felt like his last hour on earth.

"Can you please help me, John?" Tadhg pleaded, and although the last time John had seen this man they were fighting in the moonlight, he felt sorry for him.

"I'll try talk to them", John replied, showing him the open palms of his hands like the Sacred Heart, knowing that whatever was about to happen, it was out of his control.

The Holy Father pulled up a chair next to Tadhg and rolled up the sleeves of his almost white shirt. The sun shone on his back as he pulled up his trouser legs and cleared his throat. He placed one of his large hands on his knee to steady himself.

"Say your prayers and talk to me in confessional, or the next man you'll be looking at will be Saint Peter at the big black gates. Start sur. Bless me father for I have...c'mon...your last chance."

"Bless me Father for I have sinned, it's been three weeks..." Tadhg started, anything that this man wanted, he got. He had never seen this side of Peter Mulligan. His eyes were cold, weary and tired, and although he was afraid to look into them directly, what he could see was his own impending death.

"Don't worry about your last confession when your penance was three Hail Marys and two Our Fathers, this is the important one, here and now, and I will know if you're lying, and that will be the end of it, are you with me?" Peter urged him to go on.

"Bless me Father" he started again, and Peter pushed him through the monotonous part with a roll of his hand, like a conductor dictating the tempo of the orchestra.

"I have been working with the Guards for four years and feeding information to Tom and Mick."

"I'll stop you there", Peter said.

"What did you know of Augaweel, and remember, I'll know if you're lying."

"We were looking for Dinny Hegarty, that's all I know, and he's being watched as we speak, in Clonmany, by the boys in the North. Any car of interest in the Parish is bugged, including yours."

Peter was concerned about the bug but not surprised. If the Altar Boy knew, then it was an open secret of his activities away from the bar.

"Keep going", Peter placed his hand on Tadhg's shoulder.

"They know about the poteen den in Augaweel and the company you keep."

"Did you inform them for the raid on Ted Hagen's place, and remember, I know, so keep this a true confession".

"It was me, I thought he was selling from a supplier in the North. They cut me loose after they found nothing, I am dead to them now."

"You'll be dead to us as well unless you do exactly as you're told", Peter added.

"I will make you one offer that will be hard to refuse. You get to walk away from here, pack your bags and thumb a lift to Killybegs, never looking back. If you should look back, even in the rear-view mirror, I will know. If you speak to another Guard for the remainder of your life, I will know, and if this conversation gets back to me, there will not be enough corners of the world to hide in, and you will die the death of a thousand screams. Am I making sense to you yet? Now, go in peace, to love and serve the world, with a humble and contrite heart and I absolve you from your sins, in the name of the Father, Son and Holy Ghost."

Peter spoke with authority, but there was a level of compassion mixed in, as if making allowances for Tadhg growing up without a father, being spoilt by his mammy, sitting too close to the TV and the ridicule of his God-given long nose and short legs.

"Do you accept?" Peter asked finally.

"Gladly", the Altar Boy replied, breaking down in tears at being allowed to live. He looked across at John, who had kept a close watch on proceedings but far enough away to not hear the confession. TirConnell habits die hard, and it was none of his business what scrapings came off Tadhg's soul. There was enough dirt on the poteen man's street already without a barrow load of soot to go with it.

Tadhg was free to leave. His dream of being a Guard would never be realised, but he was alive. His act of contrition had saved his life, but it was more than that. He felt free and his chest was warm, like a porpoise in Lough Swilly stranded on the sand, waiting for the tide and freedom to go where he wanted, no boundaries, no gates, no nets and no ridicule of his height or look. It was as if the Holy Father had actually absolved him, and he looked forward to his new life with a clear mind. He limped across to John and put out his hand. John took it and smiled.

"Good luck Tadhg, and don't take this the wrong way, but I hope to never see you again."

John stood up as they shook hands, and he towered over his nemesis. Giving him a hug would be going too far, but he was right, and his wish was realised. They never met in person again but would watch each other's lives from afar with great interest.

"Likewise," Tadhg replied. He felt the egg-sized bump on his forehead and wondered if that was the reason for his change of heart or the threat of death from the Holy Father, either way, he felt like he had died in the crash and another soul had stepped right in and claimed his black features and short stature, thankful for the breath in his lungs and the years of life ahead of him. Tadhg walked out the lane and headed back towards Buncrana, leaving his ex-Garda car for the scrap man.

Chapter 28

The new Tadhg Byrne stood at the iron bridge with a modest sized brown bag on the pavement next to him. It was humiliating, yet if he forgot that he ever lived here, and the people staring at him were strangers from a big city, then there was nothing to be ashamed of. He needed a lift. Simple, and he stuck out his thumb to the passing cars. Tom and Mick drove past and had to do a double take. They reversed back on the side of the road and the back passenger door opened as the petrol fumes rose from the exhaust like the chimney stack at McCarter's factory. Tadhg ignored the open door, the thought of the Holy Father having him under surveillance until he got to Letterkenny at least was a very real possibility. The two Guards sat stoney faced, looking straight ahead, waiting, but a deal was a deal, and the new man would never utter another word to them. Ass's Teeth reached back and pulled the passenger door closed. It slammed shut, like any well-oiled, new car door would do. It wasn't lost on the ex-Altar Boy, and with one back door closing, another front door opened, and he looked forward to his new life.

Tadhg did make it to Killybegs and it was the best thing that ever happened. After walking around the docks for a week, he finally plucked up the courage to speak with the men. They seemed happy and how hard could it be, these boats were built for the rough seas. Within a month he was a deckhand and quickly learnt about mateship and looking after each other. He thanked the Holy Father every morning for turning his life around and for life itself.

Paddy continued to make the best poteen in Donegal, a claim that he repeated to anyone who would listen and, although there were a few minor raids from the boys in blue, for the most part, he was left alone to allow his legend status to grow and his van to become a good car, and eventually, the best car in Donegal.

Dinny got moved a further three times with the help of the Holy Father before an amnesty was called and he could return home across the border without looking over his shoulder. He never forgot the people that helped him and returned every summer holidays with his wife and weans.

John tried to keep his promise to Betty and stay at home, but he knew it wouldn't be easily kept. He continued the news in the car shed until one morning, Old Jack lay cold and still in his bed with Charlie the po laying empty. Two weeks after Old Jack had passed, a brand-new TV, the likes of which had never been seen before in Keelogs or anywhere else, arrived, courtesy of Jack and the sale of his last lot of bullocks. Liam couldn't believe the colours, and with the new aerial pointed towards Rathmullan, it was exactly what the man on the first broadcast told Ireland: it was *a window with which to view the world.*

John left for London the day that the new Tadhg Byrne got married in Killybegs. Betty cried for Ireland and again stared at the tattered suitcase by the front door. She remonstrated with the sacred heart in the kitchen, why could he not stay? But Jesus looked down, his face fitting in her despair, showing the palms of his nail damaged hands, telling her that she only held her children for a fleeting moment in time, and to hold any of them back, would be like keeping a bird in a cage: nice to look at and to while the days away with, but the bird would never be happy, never be free. Betty wiped the tears from her eyes with the back of her hand. Liam was addicted to the new TV now and sat close, far too close but it was a good distraction as John walked down the lane, like the rest of them, saying he would be home soon when he had a wheen of pound gathered up.

I stood there with the Queen, under the ash tree as he walked past. She held out her arms and John embraced her, like he had done with his mother. She sent him from this magical place with more love than I can describe here. I stood in the background, always in the background, and, in that instant, he called my name and could see me. I shook his hand and wished him well on his many journeys, knowing too that he had been raised to leave, and he would never live here again.

Liam ran to the foot of the lane as the bag was loaded in the boot of the taxi. He cried and held his brother tightly, like he would never let go, like a mother in the home that lost her boy twice. The Queen cried with Betty, cried TirConnell tears, and although this had to be, was meant to be, she marvelled at the love and broken hearts. While John's heart would never leave Keelogs,

Liam or Betty, there was a fully mapped out life to lead, and to stay was not an option. John had just turned eighteen.

Chapter 29

Frangipani leaves dropped from the tree in great amounts. It was the end of summer and although there were still a few yellow and white flowers, the tree had done its job for the season and kept the back of the house in shade from the southern summer sun. Kookaburra hens laughed on branches of gum trees on this most auspicious morning, and they welcomed the break from the intense heat and the cooler winter months ahead. Thirty-five years had passed since the parting at Keelogs, but somehow, it was no more than thirty-five seconds and closed eyes could still see the snow drops, the whitewashed pillars, Liam, John, Betty and the Queen, bound forever in TirConnell.

The lake resembled Lough Swilly, and although there were no waves of any Atlantic worth to carry the memory of a mother off into the distance, there was a clear rise and fall of the tide. The water ebbed and flowed peacefully, although salty and dark undercurrents dragged the water back out to sea at the top of the tide. John grew tired when he was furthest away from the jetty. His strong arms, that had served him well up to that point, could not take another stroke. Through the lowlines, the Aboriginal elders held their visitor up with the palms of their hands and they thanked him for the contribution and respect of their culture and lands.

Betty drifted off to sleep in the old people's home. Her eyes closed and her mind opened as she watched her son drift away with his life's work complete. She cradled him as if a newborn and helped the elders hold him above the water, until she too grew tired and gently let him drift away.

The Sacred Heart looked down from the gable wall of the kitchen in Keelogs. The red light under the smoky picture frame had been extinguished and the house had long since been abandoned, with even the clocks that once scurried behind the warm range having disappeared to a warmer house. Although Jesus looked past the empty clothesline hanging from the ceiling to the cold and damp floor below, the warmth in the house still remained and the spirit of Keelogs was alive and well. He sent love through his nail damaged hands to the memory of the occupants, their stories, trials and tribulations. He stood with Mother Mary to welcome John home as the curtain fell on his life.

The queen sat upright, watching the end unfold as the light faded in Tir-Connell and the sun set over the lough. She cried tears for the end of John as she knew him. She held her hands to the sky, merging with the people of the dreamtime, and welcomed the child of TirConnell into the land of the living. It was time.

Liam neither slept nor dreamt as he stared out onto Lough Swilly from his care home. There was a television playing in the background, a black, sleek television, that was a window with which to view the world, a pane of glass to while away his life. He remembered the TV in the car shed, with neither power nor sleek remote controls, but full of life, a window with which he viewed the world, his world, the world of love and happiness, the world with John Devenney in it. They met in the Australian Never Never, and rejoiced like two kindred souls, or a mother and son being reunited in an orphanage. Two from two. Their love was unbreakable, and one waited but an instant on the other as they changed roles, and lives again.

And so, I too must leave, and the light is calling. Tonight, I will drink a glass of Paddy Poteen's finest with my grandson, in the most beautiful place you could ever imagine.

Big George.

The potatoes had flowered in the summer sun. The tubers multiplied in the deep rich earth and the Queen lifted the best looking tops to try them out. The first pot was boiled gently in anticipation in the black pot that hung under the cast iron crane. The skins cracked, dry and powdery. They were placed on the table with salt and butter and raw onion as the first fresh potatoes since November. The young man appeared again and walked across the drills. He had his back to her, and she knew him, she called to him, but he carried on, waving the back of his hand in farewell as he walked towards the white mist. She called his name again, "John, are ye away?" and he was almost out of sight before he stopped and looked back. He smiled and this time, his dark eyebrows were illumined by the light. The white mist opened up and the potato field ceased to exist under the heavenly glow. "I'm away this time, farewell, I had the best time, thank you", he carried on like Betty's mother in the Atlantic, being carried off, slowly, wave by wave, until only a dot, before disappearing off the edge of the world.

The End

www.ingramcontent.com/pod-product-compliance
Lightning Source LLC
LaVergne TN
LVHW010622100826
845148LV00014B/3070

9780648415237